SOME LIKE IT HEXED

ACCIDENTALLY MAGICAL AT MIDLIFE? BOOK TWO

MELINDA CHASE

To the book lovers everywhere!
-Mel

SOME LIKE IT HEXED

Ever since that fateful knock weeks ago, I expected life to suddenly be brimming with adventure and magic…

Yet here I am, changing my cat's litter and flossing like nothing ever happened.

I mean, my best friend is a fae princess, and there's a magical bracelet fused to my body, for goodness sakes! Shouldn't *something* be different?!?

But aside from playing mediator in my pet's arguments (which they have far too often), life is pretty, *well*, boring again. And the only action I'm seeing is in my dreams with my favorite brooding Coven leader.

I know, I know.

I should be careful what I wish for, but as they say, you can't fight human nature.

But maybe I should've? Because I seem to have forgotten that adventure—*and danger*—go hand in hand.

And when that second fateful knock finally does come, it brings more adventure than I could've ever bargained for…

Some Like it Hexed *is the second book in the brand new series:* *Accidentally Magical at Midlife?* *from author Melinda Chase.*

Melinda loves writing tales that prove life—romance—and 'happily-ever-afters'—do exist beyond your twenties! Her books feature snarky, hilarious heroines and their wild adventures of mid-life self-discovery filled with mystery and romance. It's sure to please fans of traditional paranormal romance and cozy paranormal mysteries!

Callie

THE WIND SWEPT WARMLY around me as I stared down at the fluttering white dress that scantily clung to my curves.

My wrists were free from the constraints of the bracelet. Beneath me, soft grass caressed the underside of my feet. The world around me was vibrant and wild, colors that I had never seen within the confines of my human brain. Well... unless I counted that one night in college, but that was technically chemically induced.

"Come on," a solid sensual voice whispered to me.

My eyes rose, finding two bare feet hovering just above the ground. As I slowly devoured the tight leather pants leading up to the muscular, glistening, shirtless torso in front of me, I fanned myself. There he was, in all his sexy, emo, witchy man glory. Shade's mouth was upturned in a huge, toothpaste commercial-worthy smile, and I sighed dramatically, having my first ever swooning moment.

He hovered there on his expertly crafted, intricately carved broomstick. Sure, it was a stereotype. And I was pretty sure that had it been the real world and not my dream, Thorne would have been pretty pissed at the idea of himself on a broomstick. But it was *my* dream, and I wasn't about to change it and risk waking myself up.

"Hop on, we'll go for a...ride."

I swooned even harder at the sound of his voice and reached out to take his hand. It was warm and smooth, and I bit my bottom lip as my far perkier than real-life breasts pushed against the satin of my dress. As I stepped forward, and my eyes met his, he opened his mouth to grace me yet again with that low, seductive rumble... But that was not at all what I got. Instead of his voice, the sound of a deep, gurgling snore came from his throat.

Instantly, I pulled my hands into tight fists and clenched my eyes shut. "No, no, no. Do not wake up. Do. Not. Wake. Up."

I opened one eye and then the other, staring at Shade's hot, chiseled body with my basset hound's head replacing his beautiful face. He snorted as a long string of spit dripped from the corner of his sloppy jowls. My arms fell to my sides, defeated, and I let out a long, unhappy breath. "Dammit."

For the first time since Shade had left, I had a dream about something other than creepy monsters coming after me or my bracelet taking over my whole body. For the first time in weeks, I wasn't waking up in a tired sweat, unsure of where I was. And what did I get?

My dog, Bean, nudged me, his head still firmly planted on my hot-witch-dream man body, snorting. I reached up, still dreaming, and patted his head. "You really are cramping my style. When I wake up from this dream, you better not be drooling on my face."

My eyes glanced over Shade's strong muscles one last time, and I rolled my eyes, closing them once again. I could feel a trickle of cold air move up my spine as I woke in my bed, staring directly into a snoring basset hound's face. "This is my life… forty years old, finding out there's magic, and sleeping next to a basset hound as I dream of some guy on the other side of the world. Wonderful."

I groaned as I rolled away from the dog and tilted the alarm clock upward, finding it was only two in the morning at that point. I was still relatively groggy, which wasn't shocking considering I hadn't really slept well since everything had happened. Pulling the covers back over my shoulder, I nestled back in, hoping that my dream would return, but really just wishing to get some sleep. Just as I began to drift off, the sound of muffled voices echoed from outside of my room. My hands gripped tightly to the blanket, and I opened my eyes, shifting them back and forth.

I waited, wondering if maybe, just maybe, I was still halfway in my dream. Just as I was about to relax again, chalking it up to another moment of paranoia, which I'd had a lot lately, the voices rang out again, snappy and angry. Bean snorted next to me but didn't wake up. I slowly pulled back the covers and sat up, dangling my legs over the bed. My hands gripped the edge of the mattress tightly, and I could feel a tingle from the bracelet shimmering up my arm.

My eyes flickered around the room, looking for any type of weapon that I could possibly use. Sure, the bracelet had somehow chased away an evil overlord collecting kings, but it wasn't my magic. And I had zero understanding of how to control it. I nudged my dog with my elbow. "Aren't you going to get up? Don't you hear that?"

One of Bean's eyes opened, and he sniffed the air. "Ball?"

"No." I rolled my eyes and pointed toward the door. "Don't you hear those voices?"

Before his brain could even connect the two thoughts, he was mumbling and falling back to sleep. "Bean off-duty."

The sound came again from outside the room, and I chewed nervously on my bottom lip as I scanned the room again, looking for anything I could grab. I had a stand-up lamp, but that would be really awkward to swing in the house.

Body spray? No, not foolproof. Strangle them with a scarf? Callie, you are not a ninja.

Finally, my eyes landed on the dresser where I had tossed my cooled-down flat iron. I quietly crept over to it and grabbed it, snapping it open and closed like a lobster's claw. It would have to do.

As I carefully and quietly as I could, I crept toward the door and slowly turned the knob, letting it gently open up. I peeked down the hallway, but all I could see were dancing shadows in the dimly lit living room. I took a deep breath and opened the door the rest of the way, quickly making my way toward the voices. As if I were going to triumphantly defeat whoever was in my living room with a flat iron, the cord catching on the carpet as I dragged it behind me, I burst into the room.

"Don't talk to me like that, fleabag," Willa growled, staring down at Mr. Hobbles, who was sitting on the couch, licking his cat paw.

"Fleabag, how dare you!"

Suddenly, both my talking cat and my best friend turned to look at me, standing there in my pajamas, my hair wild, spit caked to my cheek, holding my flat iron. The fear rushed out of me, and I shook my head. "What are you guys doing? It's two o'clock in the morning."

Willa put her hands on her hips and pointed at the cat. "Your cat is a rude, disrespectful, giant ball of fur."

Mr. Hobbles gasped dramatically. "I'll have

you know, within the cat community, I am considered a top breed."

Willa rolled her eyes. "Please. I was there when she picked you out of the lineup at the pound. It took her two weeks to get the smell of trash out of your fur."

"Rags to riches," Mr. Hobbles replied, his head in the air, his British accent thicker than ever.

"Do I need to send the two of you to couples counseling? What could you possibly be arguing about at this hour?"

Willa pointed at him. "He won't get out of the spot that I need to sleep in."

Mr. Hobbles curled into a ball. "This is my spot. It has been ever since I came here. You've outworn you're welcome. Don't you have a home? Perhaps some poor defenseless creature of your own to torture?"

Willa narrowed her eyes and stepped forward, but I put up my hands and shook my head. "Enough, you two. Hobbles, you're being rude to our guest. If you don't want to end up looking like one of those hairless cats, I suggest you go find another place to sleep."

A low grumble came from the cat's chest, and he narrowed his eyes at Willa before hopping down and running off. I rolled my eyes and shook my head, plopping down onto the sofa. Willa sat next to me. We both looked at the flat iron in my hand and giggled.

Willa rubbed her hand on my back, sending a comforting warmth through my chest. "Bad dreams again?"

I tossed the flat iron onto the coffee table in front of me and rubbed my face. "No. Well... it didn't start out that way." I paused, imagining Shade with Bean's head. I shook the image from my mind. "It's been two weeks. It's been two weeks since everything happened in Rome. We came back here, and it's like I'm supposed to go on with my life. We haven't heard anything from the witches. I was literally kidnapped multiple times, taken to Rome, abducted by some crazy magical creature, and now I have your bracelet melded into my body. Oh yeah, and the fact that magic is real... It's just a lot. And it's a lot not to be answered."

Willa gave me a half-smile and nodded, folding her hands in her lap. "I know it seems like forever, but these things take time. After what you saw, and the fact that whoever it is probably knows that we've kind of joined forces in this whole thing, they're probably quiet right now. If the witches knew anything, I'm sure they'd be here to let us know."

I fell back against the couch and rolled my eyes. "I know. But how long? I keep looking over my shoulder, waiting for the next thing to happen. I keep thinking, any second now, the witches are going to land on our front doorstep with news from the witch world."

Just as I finished my sentence, there was a loud and echoing knock on the front door. I immediately sat up at the same time as Willa, our backs straight, staring over, both wondering if we had imagined the knocking. We sat very still for several moments. "You heard that, right?"

Willa nodded. "I did. And it's almost too much of a coincidence for even me."

Slowly, we looked at each other, blinking. We jumped again as a knock sounded on the door even louder than the first time. I put my hand down on the arm of the couch and lifted myself up. Willa grabbed my hand. "What are you doing?"

I pointed at the door. "I'm going to go answer that... Obviously, it's not just a salesman. We don't need them waking up the whole neighborhood."

Deep down, I was hoping it would be Shade, though the reasoning for that I wasn't exactly sure yet. I wasn't positive that it didn't have to do with that dream I had just had. At the same time, I was desperate for answers and for things to move forward. I was tired of living in limbo, replaying the events in Rome over and over again in my head.

Willa slowly let go of my hand. "Be careful."

I lifted a brow at her. "If somebody's gonna come after us, they're not going to just knock on the front door."

Willa pursed her lips. "Really? Did you already forget what happened to you last time? You were literally kidnapped after somebody knocked on the front door."

I paused but then shook my head. "That was your front door."

I wasn't going to lie. There was a certain level of anxiety rumbling around my stomach. Whoever was on the other side of the door wasn't going to leave. As I approached the door and reached out for the handle, I glanced back at Willa. She was standing about three feet behind me, her shoulders stiff, gripping the flat iron in both hands.

"You could've at least plugged this in on turbo

mode or something…." Willa said, touching the cold ceramic plates.

"Really? I'm sorry. I'm sure that the bag guys I thought were breaking into my house would definitely have allowed me three minutes to heat up my flat iron before attacking. Hell, maybe we could have had a little makeover session before they tried to kill me with their magic."

Willa rolled her eyes, and the knock sounded again. I turned back and took a deep breath, pushing the fear out of me, not wanting to show Willa—who was more nervous than I had seen her in a while—that my knees would be smacking together if I wasn't consciously trying to keep everything from shaking. I opened the door just a crack, paused for a moment, and then swung it wide. Standing on the other side were the two fae bodyguards who had, just a few weeks before, kidnapped me, taking me on a wild car ride, and then left me with the witches. This time though, they had ditched the I Love San Fran T-shirts and were dressed in white flowing tunics, matching pants, and sandals. Their eyes were a beautiful crystal blue, and they looked exactly how I imagined the fae would look.

I put my hands on my hips and narrowed my eyes at them. "Did you guys not get the memo?

You do know we've done this already, right?" I looked back at Willa. "Is this like one of those glitches in the matrix?"

Her eyes shifted from me back to the guys, but her facial expression changed. Slowly, I turned back to see what she was looking at, finding a tall, beautiful fae woman stepping between the guards. She had long, glistening, amber hair that rolled over her shoulders and down her back. Her eyes were that same beautiful crystal blue, her skin very fair, and her lips pink. She moved slowly and gracefully, and when she smiled at me, it was as if a warm blanket were wrapped around me. The fae woman's eyes then shifted behind me, but her smile stayed. "Hello, Willa. It's been a long time."

I turned on my heels to face Willa and watched as her eyes went wide and her mouth dropped, the flat iron falling from her hand. Her stare stayed glued to the fae woman.

"Aunt Liza, what are you doing here?"

2

Callie

I STOOD TO THE SIDE, holding the door as Willa's gorgeous fae aunt practically glided into the room.

She was wearing a beautiful, basically see-through dress with intricate, heavy beading. However, it looked like it weighed almost nothing. The first guard to pass me had been the driver when I was kidnapped, and he didn't even attempt to make eye contact. The second one, however…oh boy.

His eyes immediately narrowed, and I winced, seeing the remnants of what looked like two black eyes and a crease across his perfect fae nose. His glare could have cut me to the very pit of my soul if I weren't careful.

I giggled nervously. "Sorry about that."

The first guard turned back and chuckled, grabbing the second by his arm and pulling him into the house. I rolled my eyes and puffed my cheeks, realizing that just when I thought life couldn't get any more awkward, in walk the two fae guards, I practically beat up in the middle of traffic. When I began to shut the door, a hand came from the doorway and stopped me. My heart raced as my eyes lifted to see Shade, standing there just as I had remembered him... Well, this time with a shirt on and definitely not with my dog's head on his shoulders.

He flashed me a smirk as his dark eyes met mine. My heart did some sort of pretzel flip twist in my chest, and I swallowed hard. Behind him, his main guard, Thorne, strutted in. He gave me a mischievous grin and hurried inside. I stood there slightly shocked and definitely taken off guard. As everyone gathered in the living room, I shut and locked the door, making sure the drapes were fully closed. It was quite the sight to see. Four fae, including Willa, stood in my house with two witches.

Thorne eyed the two fae guards, and I could see the distrust float between them. Thorne thumbed at the second fae guard, glancing over at me. "Is this the one you roughed up in the car? Damn girl. Maybe you have a little witch in you after all."

The first guard put his hand on the second's chest and gave him a look. Willa was still staring at her Aunt Liza in disbelief, but that only lasted until Shade cleared his throat and began to talk. "We came…"

Willa shook her head and put up her hands, casting an angered glare in Shade's direction. "Hold up. Wait one second. I know that the witches believe they owe no one any type of explanation, but you and I had an understanding. No one was supposed to go to the fae realm except for me. What made you think you had the right…"

Willa's aunt put up her hand, and immediately Willa fell quiet. I wasn't used to seeing her caged so easily. The dynamic between her and her aunt brought up a lot of questions in my mind.

"They didn't cross into the fae realm. In fact, it was I who came to them to ask permission to cross realms."

As her aunt talked, a simmering type of energy ran up my arm. It was different than before, leaving a fiery sensation on my skin. I rubbed my hand up and down my arm, trying to ignore the feeling.

Willa furrowed her brow. "What? Why?"

Liza gracefully glided over to the couch, looked at it curiously for a moment, and took a seat on the edge of the cushion. Pretentious wasn't really a good description of how she was behaving. Her actions were closer to careful than anything else. It wasn't like I blamed her. Between Bean and Hobbles, the place had enough fur to knit sweaters for the entire fae realm. Every time I turned around, one of them was rubbing themselves across the furniture. I knew Bean did it because he had itchy skin and didn't think twice about relieving the itch on anything he came across. Mr. Hobbles, on the other hand, was a jerk, and I didn't put it past him to spread his fur just because he knew Willa had to sleep there.

Aunt Liza placed her patient hands in her lap and looked up at everyone. "When I crossed over and met with Shade, I was told about the things that have happened here with you. I was told that my men got here in time, but unfortunately, the witches were mistaken. However, I don't necessarily see that as a bad thing."

Her eyes shifted to me. "We have learned of the King Collector, as well as the dangers that we were not aware had been released."

Willa nodded. "From what Callie told us, there are creatures I've never heard of. I know I've been gone a while, but whatever is out there, it's not something I believe takes a stroll down Main Street daily."

Liza shook her head. "No, but there are realms even the fae have not experienced. This creature could be from anywhere. There have been historical writings of creatures in dark robes roaming the Forests of Elm, but none that we've ever physically seen."

Listening, I noticed Willa wring her hands at the sound of the Forests of Elm. She swallowed hard, and it was visibly noticeable that her mind had wandered off to another event and back again. It was curious, and I made a mental note to ask her about it later. Eventually, Willa shook the haze from her eyes and began to pace back and forth. "So, is that why you crossed over? I mean, you could have sent one of the guards to talk with us about that. With my father missing…well, I figured you'd be pretty busy."

Liza sighed and stood, walking over to the fireplace mantel. She scanned the photos of my family and me and then turned back to Willa. The smile on her face was gone, and that searing tingle spun up my arm. Without control, I hissed, grabbing my arm. Everyone looked over at me. Slowly, I let go of my arm and smiled, trying not to turn the conversation to me. "I'm fine."

Everyone but Shade turned back to Willa. He, however, narrowed his eyes at me and scrunched his forehead as if he were trying to speak to me telepathically.

Was that a thing?

If it were, I wasn't in on it. I lightly shook my head and turned back, trying to ignore the heat surging up the back of my neck, just knowing Shade was staring at me.

"I've taken over as queen regent while your father is missing. You were, naturally, the next in line of power, but we knew your instructions were specific. Then, when we had attempted to come to get you…that didn't turn out as we hoped." Aunt Liza glanced over at her guards, but they stood tall, their eyes straight ahead, ignoring the snickering from Thorne.

"Right," Willa replied. "I understand. But it's been thousands of years since you've crossed realms. Why not just send your guards again. Maybe this time tell them not to dress in strange San Francisco tourist outfits."

Liza nodded. "Understood. I had planned to make the trip in person anyway. I haven't seen you in so long—my sweet sister's daughter. And I wanted the news of the kidnapping of your father to come from me. I had planned to speak to the emissary between realms to organize that visit for me, but then something else happened, and I couldn't wait."

Willa unfolded her hands, and I could see her shoulders straighten. "What happened? Did you find my father?"

"No," she sighed. "The Stone of Stars was stolen the night before last."

Willa's mouth dropped open, and she put her hand back, feeling around for the chair before her legs gave way, and she plopped down. "That's... that's..."

"A disaster," Liza replied, "and that's putting it lightly."

Willa nodded, her eyes shifted down, her

mind obviously roaming around the words her aunt had just spoken. She blinked her eyes several times, and she breathed deeply. "What do you need from me?"

Liza placed her hands together again, and the smile returned to her face. "We need you in the fae realm. You have always been so loved, and with your return, I believe we can keep the fae calm when this eventually gets out."

"Who knows?"

Liza pressed her lips together. "The main heads of state know. Now the witches know, but that's it. Even the staff in the fae castle were kept in the dark. I put a replica in its place, so the guards didn't notice."

"They haven't seen me in…a very long time. I was a little girl mourning the death of her mother," Willa replied. "I'm not sure how much I can help in that aspect."

"I believe you're wrong," Liza replied. "And plus, I really need your help finding your father and the stone."

Shade crossed his arms over his chest. "Do you believe it's the same person involved?"

Liza looked over her shoulder at Shade. "I have no idea. Whoever this is, they leave no clues behind. Not a single hair or magical trace. I won't rule it out."

Willa pursed her lips. "Right. Okay. I guess I can't say no to that."

Liza turned toward me and nodded. "Callie, having you there will be a huge help as well."

Slightly thrown off, I pointed at myself. "Me? Um, okay. But what is this stone? Why does it seem even worse than Willa's father missing?"

"Because the stone is everything to the fae," Shade replied. "It's the past, present, and future."

I blinked at him. "Riiiight. That's not really clear to me. Talk to me like I'm a human that just found out that there really is magic and my best friend is a fae."

Liza smiled. "The stone is a beacon for the fae. It is the singular point from which our world and our magic came from. It was much larger, obviously, at the beginning of our world, but it's relatively small now. There's only one other small piece of that stone remaining, and we have to keep it out of the hands of whoever took the larger stone."

I nodded. "Okay. I see that this stone is definitely important, but what does that have to do with me?"

Liza's eyes shifted down, and I followed her

gaze to the bracelet on my wrist. I turned my hand over, palm up, and found a glistening purple and blue stone shimmering and flickering on my wrist.

Well…shit.

3

Callie

"THE WITCHES NEED to be there, too," Shade said, breaking me from my trance.

I was still trying to wrap my mind around the fact that I had a piece of a stone on my wrist that created the entirety of the fae realm. I could only assume that had something to do with the tingling sensation constantly running up and down my arms. Either way, the power of it was overwhelming.

Shade's voice was a nice break of thought. "We have a right to be there."

Liza turned toward Shade, and that smile that had initially felt so warm and comforting suddenly felt more condescending and fake as each moment passed. A bit of irritation surged in my chest at the way she was snidely glaring at Shade, but I did my best to keep the bitch expression off of my face.

"I'm not sure that's a good idea," she replied.

Shade put out his hand, catching Thorne over the chest before he could speak. Shade's eyes stayed glued to Liza's, and his expression was still and unmoving. "While I appreciate the rarity of witches in the fae realm, there is more at stake here than just your king."

"And bringing your kind to our realm isn't going to help that situation," she replied with a steady tone.

Thorne opened his mouth to speak, and Shade threw him a furious look. Thorne immediately backed up, but his stance was anything but friendly. Shade's hands twitched at his sides. "Our kind?"

"You heard the queen," one of the guards barked angrily.

Sparks began to simmer at the tips of Thorne's fingers, and the two guards reached behind their backs. Suddenly everything became very still. Visions of a shoot-out with bullets and magic raced through my head. My eyes immediately shot over to Willa, pleading with her to say something to calm the situation.

She got the hint pretty quickly. "Aunt Liza, Shade was there when Callie was abducted, he and his men put their lives on the line to save her, and they have been helping to track this being down. Shade would be an asset to us in the search for both my father and the stone. He is not a threat to us. His brother, the king of the witches, has been abducted, too."

Willa's aunt pursed her lips and put her hands up, glancing at her guards. They glared at Thorne for a moment and then relaxed, pulling their hands back in front of them. Shade glanced at Thorne, and he pulled his magic back into himself.

Liza looked Shade up and down for several moments. "Since my niece is very insistent on your coming with us, I will allow it."

Shade nodded.

"*But,*" Liza continued, "just you. It's going to be hard enough hiding a human much less more than one witch in the fae realm."

"Hide us?" I asked.

Willa glanced over. "Technically, humans

25

aren't supposed to know about magic. And witches haven't crossed into our realms in thousands of years. You'll have a spell over you to help you blend in with our people a bit better. The bracelet will help you a lot, but Shade will need some work. Fae can smell a witch a mile away."

Liza sneered and then stood up. "I will allow you to get your affairs in order. Whatever you have here in this world, put it on hold. You may be in the fae realm for a while."

I didn't like the sound of that at all. Sure, visiting sounded exciting, but for an unknown amount of time? I would just have to deal with it. I needed to help Willa find her father. And I needed Shade to find his brother. Everything would be pointless if those two things didn't happen. I would just have to figure out the bracelet issue later.

Liza put out her hand to the guard, who reached into his pocket and pulled out a tiny, rolled scroll.

The queen regent walked over to Willa and set it in her palm. "Do not be late. You know I cannot leave the portal open. If you don't come through, it may be a long time before I can organize this again."

"Yes, ma'am," Willa replied.

Liza smiled at her and leaned down, kissing her forehead. As she turned, she glanced down at my bracelet, and I could feel a sharp spike race up my arm. I gripped my fist tightly closed but kept my facial expression as straight as possible. For a moment, I thought she was going to reach out and touch my wrist, but she pulled back her hand and walked toward the door, her guards following behind her. I didn't turn to watch them leave. I was too busy trying not to make a face. I didn't know why the bracelet was acting differently around her, but it was a bit more than suspicious to me.

But what could I do?

If I told Shade, he would be suspicious, and with the pressure on him already, going to the fae realm, I didn't want to add fuel to that fire. And Willa...well, I couldn't tell her that her aunt was giving off some crazy bracelet vibes. It was her family. I would just keep it to myself, and hopefully, it would subside.

I watched Willa's shoulders fall in relief as the front door closed. She reached into her pocket and texted someone. "Let's head over to the *Lustrous Bean*. We have a lot to do in a short amount of time. Plus, I want to update the others on what's going on. We'll need someone to stay be-

27

hind and run the shop, but let's make sure it's easy on them."

I nodded, glancing over at Shade before slipping off to my room to get out of the pajamas I just realized I was wearing and into a pair of yoga pants and a T-shirt. I had a feeling I wouldn't be wearing my regular comfort clothes in the fae realm. With the work we had to get done before the next night, I needed to make sure I was comfortable. As much as Shade made me anxious, he also gave off a comforting vibe that I hadn't noticed in him before. But maybe it wasn't magic like it was for Willa. Perhaps I had just gotten comfortable with him. Either way, it saved me time not freaking out over pulling my hair back into a ponytail and grabbing a zip-up hoodie.

When I was done, I headed back out to the living room where Willa was waiting for me. I glanced around nonchalantly, but Shade and Thorne weren't there anymore.

"They're already heading over to the coffee shop to make sure it's safe before we get there," Willa said as if she could read my mind.

I nodded as if it weren't even a question in my mind, and I could see the slight smirk on her lips. She turned to say something to me, and I shook my head. "If it's about Shade, don't."

With a grin, she put up her hands, turning to walk toward the door. "I'm not going to fight you on that. I know I'm going to have a big enough fight from the four fae who will be waiting for us when we get to the shop. I know though they'll want to go home, they've been away for a very long time. But I'm going to need two of them to stay behind."

Then and only then did it dawn on me that not only was I going to the fae realm for the first time, but Willa was headed back to her home. She was headed back to a place that she had left a long time before and built a life somewhere else. It was a place that, to Willa, there was plenty of hurt and sadness. It dawned on me that Willa would take the reins of her father, stepping in as the ruler of the entire fae realm. The magnitude of that was hard for me to fathom, much less Willa finding herself in this position out of nowhere.

Everything was about to change, and waiting for us in a realm I had never been, was an enemy, maybe more than one, that looked to end the fae world and everything in it.

Oh boy, a whole new set of pressures. Time to strap on the heavy-duty yoga pants.

4

Shade

STANDING on the sidewalk outside of the café, the sun just starting to come up over the horizon, I could see the violent waves crashing against the shore in the distance.

It was a beautiful place, I couldn't deny that, and I could see why Callie was so attached to the place she grew up. But every time I started to enjoy something, find comfort in it, my brother, Vlad, pushed through my mind. I didn't know where he was, but I could still see his face from the vision I had been shown just a couple weeks before. I had to find him, and if it took going to the fae realm, then so be it.

"All right, everything's spelled, and we should be good," Thorne said, coming around the side of the building and standing next to me on the sidewalk. "Look, I'd be a terrible guard and best friend if I didn't say this. I think it's bull shit that I can't go with you. I think you should have fought for it. Going to the fae realm right now is the worst thing you could do. I know you were born to be a king. Your brother is gone, and you have an entire coven spread out across the world that's looking to you for answers."

I tore my gaze away from the ocean and put my hand on Thorne's shoulder, giving him a smile. "And I can't find my brother without doing this. That's why I'm putting somebody I trust in command."

Thorne raised a brow. "Who?"

I chuckled, squeezing his shoulder. "You, fool. I want you to run things to make sure everybody is safe while I'm gone. I will return. And if I have any luck left in me at all, I'll be returning with my brother. In the meantime, the witches need to stay safe, and I can't think of anybody better than you to keep them that way."

Thorne's chin came up just a bit, and I could

see the pride in his eyes. He put one hand across his stomach and bent forward, bowing. "It's a great honor. I won't let you down. But I still don't think you should go to the fae realm. I'm telling you, there's something about that queen regent that I just don't trust."

"How does it feel?" a voice said from behind us.

We turned to find the four fae who had traveled with Willa standing with their arms crossed outside the coffee shop. Esmeralda, the older one, usually quiet and strange, looked much more brazen as she tapped her foot, waiting for a response.

Thorne narrowed his eyes and glanced at me but thankfully kept his cool. "How does what feel?"

"Being forced to work with somebody you don't trust? It's tough, isn't it?"

We could both see what she was getting at, and before there could be any replies, Willa and Callie drove up, parking their SUV outside of the shop. As they jumped from the truck, Willa paused, looking back and forth between Thorne and the other fae.

"Oh good, still getting along, I see. Come on, we've got things to do."

I let Willa and Callie take the fae into the shop, and I turned and stopped Thorne from following. "I need you to get back to the castle. I'll let you know when I've returned."

"And if you don't? Who do I hold responsible?"

I stared at my kind friend, knowing he meant that with the utmost respect for my life. "I can tell you who not to hold responsible. I know that Callie and Willa won't have anything to do with it. And don't judge the queen regent too quickly. We both know the fae are strange beings, and it isn't abnormal for us to instantly not trust them. Just keep that simmering in the back of your head. And Thorne? Thank you."

Thorne nodded, and I stepped back, watching as he gave me a massive grin before disappearing. I glanced up and down the street to make sure nobody had seen that, but everything was still closed and quiet. Turning and walking up to the glass windows of the coffee shop, I could see Willa talking to the fae, Callie standing nervously in the background. She was staring down at her bracelet, and I knew she was worried about the stone within it. To be honest, now knowing what was powering the bracelet helped me understand where the magic was coming from when it came to Callie. At least a little bit.

I quietly slipped inside and locked the door behind me, leaning against one of the bookcases as they talked. I wasn't really the one who had anything to do with Willa's coffee shop or their business at all.

Callie meandered over next to me. "I'm glad you're coming to the fae world. I hope we can find your brother."

My eyes shifted to hers. I couldn't help notice the rosiness of her cheeks and feel the proximity of her body next to mine. There was an awkward uncomfortableness between us, but it wasn't necessarily a bad thing. It was an emotion that I hadn't felt in a very long time, but it was also one that I would have to push away. There was no time for me to have any kind of romantic relationship with anyone. It was just hard with Callie because I felt pulled to her. We were like two magnets.

Before I could reply to her, Willa's voice faded out, and the fae began to talk amongst themselves. We watched as Willa hugged Esmeralda and Harry and made her way over to us.

"Everything set?"

Willa nodded, but I could see the nervousness behind her eyes.

Callie waved to Esmeralda and Harry, turning to Willa, confused. "Where are they going?"

"Esmeralda was my mother's hand, and she's going to return with me to take that place until we can come back. Harry's going to come along with us. They're going to go get their things in order and meet us at the portal."

Callie nodded. "And the other two? They're going to stay here and run the shop?"

Willa nodded but didn't say anymore.

"Thank you for sticking up for me with your aunt. I do want you to know that it's just as much of a priority to me to find your father as it is my brother. With the stone missing, I can see how this will begin to affect every realm, including our own." While we both knew that my words were in thanks and that, in reality, my brother was my top priority, I felt it essential that Willa knew we were on the same side.

I knew what it was like to step into a role that was never meant for me, and I knew that she was struggling through it.

"So, where's this portal we'll be leaving from?" Callie asked.

Willa pulled out the small scroll and unrolled it. "The South Pier at exactly 11:52 PM, to-morrow night. We've got a lot of work to do.

Why don't you go back and start taking stock of the room, and I'll get some orders done?"

"You? Do the ordering?" Callie giggled, and the sound of it struck me at my core. "I'm pretty sure we still have things leftover from the special order you did at the beginning of the year."

I could see the trademark fae sparkling shimmer in Willa's eyes again. "I think for this situation, having a bit of excess isn't going to hurt anyone." She turned her attention to me. "And you're welcome. I'm going to need all the help that I can get. And keeping Callie safe is one of my top priorities."

"I will do whatever I can," I replied.

I stood there at the bookshelf, watching as Willa and Callie split off, Callie standing behind the register and Willa heading to the back stock room. I could remember the days where adventures like the one we were about to undertake would've made me almost giddy with excitement. However, going to the fae realm, where I was already considered an enemy, coupled with the danger Callie was under, a feeling of dread settled deep in the pit of my stomach. It was a world I hadn't been to in a very long time, a world that had no regard for my life or Callie's. I really hoped that whatever happened there, we find my brother and I could get Callie back safely.

Whatever role Callie was meant to play in all of this, with the fae involved, I knew it could either turn out really well, or we were in for the fight of our life.

5

Callie

I STEPPED through the swinging doors to the stockroom, and as soon as it closed behind me, I put out my hand and rested on the boxes stacked to my right. Letting my head hang, I took in a couple of deep breaths, trying to center myself.

From the moment I opened the door and saw Willa's aunt standing there, I was holding it back. I was holding back fear, excitement, questions, and everything else that went along with magic suddenly dropping back into my lap two weeks later.

And then there was Shade.

He hadn't really said anything to me, but just having his presence there made me feel better. I knew there was something between us, but he was tough to read. It looked like, though, I would have plenty of time to get to know him better in the coming weeks. I grabbed the clipboard off the wall and held it up, blowing the excess glitter off the paper. Every checklist, every advertisement, every notepad was covered in some sort of glittery concoction that Willa crafted herself during the quiet hours at the coffee shop.

As the tiny specks of sparkling paper fluttered to the floor, I thought about times before I knew about all the magic. I thought about all the quiet days and even quieter nights. I thought about my obsession with having a safe life and how quickly that had completely turned upside down. For the first time in years, I hadn't stopped to think about my parents every single day. I was too busy trying to figure out how to stay alive to think about that kind of thing. It was kind of a win for me, though. It wasn't that I wanted to forget them, but I definitely needed to move forward. I just didn't think that moving forward meant ahead through a portal into another realm. I thought more like taking a yoga class and maybe going out to the bar once a month.

I rolled my shoulders, letting the thought pass by me. There was no use in thinking about it over and over again. Things were what they were, and now what I had to focus on was leaving behind my life for an undisclosed amount of time and hoping that it was there when I got back. Actually, my first hope was that *I* would be there to come back.

I dragged my feet over to the first rack of coffee-related items and began to go down the checklist. Almost everything in the stockroom was overstocked, keeping me from having to place an order every single week. Every time Willa did the order, we ended up with not enough coffee beans and far too much random flavoring or sparkly edible glitter. All things that would sit on the shelf until either we magically went through them or they expired and I tossed them out.

This time though, it wasn't a matter of making do. I wanted to make sure there was enough of everything to get Bella and Cruz through the next several weeks, at least. I was glad that Bella was staying to help run the shop. She had been the one person who had actually taken over for Willa and me a couple of times when we went out of town for an event or decided to take a day off together. She knew the gist of running the place, and she was a smart girl. She would have no problem, and I had no problem trusting her with the store.

While going to see the fae realm was exciting in some ways, not knowing how long I would be there took a lot of that excitement away. I hoped that I would get back soon, but more importantly, I hoped that I would come back alive. Ever since I was a little girl, I dreamed of a realm of fae, but after meeting Willa's aunt, I was less excited than I was before. For some reason, I had worked up the fae in my mind to be these beings that lacked every negative trait that humans possessed and had all the beautiful aspects, plus magic. However, after seeing the looks between witches and fae and how Willa's aunt was incredibly condescending, I wondered if the fae realm was just a magical version of earth.

The door swung open behind me, and I glanced over my shoulder, finding Shade walking in, looking around the cluttered and piled room. "You actually have to order things? It looks like you have enough stuff here to last the shop for at least a couple years."

I rolled my eyes and chuckled, checking off another box on the spreadsheet. "We can thank Willa and her absolutely devastating ordering abilities for a lot of the stuff. It's not really usable, not on a daily basis. If we're leaving and we don't know when we're coming back, I want to make sure that all the normal everyday stuff is fully stocked."

He walked up next to me and stared up at the coffee beans. "Are you nervous about going to the fae realm?"

"Nervous?" I replied, reaching out and pushing one of the rows of coffee beans to the left. "I'm not really nervous, but I'm excited. I've never been to a place like that. I mean, I just realized it was a place two weeks ago."

When Shade didn't immediately respond, I glanced up at him and found him chewing on the inside of his cheek, staring blankly at the row of creamer in front of him. "I feel like I should say something. Look, the fae realm is not as amazing as you would think. I was born and raised here on Earth, so I have a really good idea of what human beings believe the fae world would be like. And for all intents and purposes, on the outside, it's a lot of what humans think it is. It's beautiful, secluded, and generally peaceful. But the fae aren't these creatures above all others like they're portrayed in so many human stories. They aren't always the hero. They face the same kind of decisions and issues that humans do. They just get to use magic to help."

I turned toward him, watching his face. Something was going on, something more than what he was leading me to believe. "It's obvious that there's something about the fae world that you don't like. Did something happen there?"

Shade closed his eyes for a moment, and I wondered where he was going. His mind fluttered off to some other place and then came back. "There's a lot of darkness inside the fae realm. That darkness stretches outward into the community but also deeply into the royal court. I assume part of the reason why Willa left the way she did was because of that darkness within the royal hierarchy."

I took a deep breath and shrugged. "I guess if you really think about it, if the fae world were the way that it's depicted in human stories and movies, it would be kind of boring after a little while. While I am excited to see the place, I don't have any real expectations for the fae world to be much different after the things that I've seen the last month. What's most important to me is that we help find Willa's father, the stone, and your brother. I'd like to do that with as little complication from the fae as possible."

He snickered. "Good luck with that. The Fae Council has a reputation for trying to control everything within their realm." He paused, and his voice lowered as his eyes shifted around the room. "When I was a kid, my brother and I went to the fae realm as part of my brother's celebrations leading to his coronation as king. It sounds fancy but what it really represents is the connection between magical communities for continued alliance and peace."

I nodded, listening intently.

"My brother, he was always soft-spoken, kind, and not at all what you would assume a king of the witches to really be like. I had always been his protector and gave him the courage to stand up for what he believed and what he knew was right. When we were younger, he always insisted that I stay in the same room as him. It was our last night. We had already met with the Fae Council and participated in their traditional dinners and events. We were slated to come back to Earth the next day. During the night, someone came into our room. I woke up, finding them lurking in the shadows. They lunged at my brother, holding a magical dagger. I threw myself at them, struggled with them, and eventually, they ran off. My brother woke up and thanked me but then realized I was bleeding."

On instinct, my hand came to my mouth, and I watched him pat his lower stomach.

"I almost died," he said quietly. "My brother had always been really gifted with healing magic, and before my father could even get the room, he had stopped the bleeding and closed the wound."

"Did they ever catch who it was?" I asked.

Shade shook his head. "No. Just like what's going on now, whoever it was, they were really good at covering their tracks. Willa's father was very upset, but none of the investigations they did ever came back with anything. My father always thought it was someone within the council, but not someone like Willa's father. I promised my father before he passed away that I would always watch out for my brother. But now he's out there, and there's no one to protect him."

Without thought, I reached out and touched his arm, moving closer to him. "With as strong as it sounds like you've been for him and all the things you've done to protect him, I'm sure he learned a few things from you. My only experience with royalty to this point is a TV series on the queen of England. But just to stand there as your leader, as the king, takes an incredible amount of courage. I'm sure your brother is holding onto that right now. We'll find him. And we'll find Willa's father as well."

He smiled at me kindly and lifted his hand, running it over my shoulder and down my arm. I couldn't tell whether the tingles going up and down my arm were from the bracelet or Shade's touch, but whatever it was, I never wanted it to stop. Standing in a dusty coffee shop backroom wasn't the most romantic thing I had ever done. Despite the lack of magic involved, it was the most fantastic feeling since I was tied to two wooden posts, minus the whole fearing for my life thing, of course.

The space between us began to close, and our eyes stayed locked on each other. Everything around us was so still. All I could hear was the beating of my heart. I longed to kiss his lips, to feel his arms tugging me closer to his warm, hard body. There was something about him that pulled me in like a magnet.

"Hey, Callie," Willa shouted out as she came

bursting through the stockroom doors, looking down at one of her lists.

Immediately, Shade and I jumped back from each other, and I nervously tugged at the end of my ponytail. Willa glanced up, but she didn't seem to notice anything going on between Shade and me. She stood next to me, looking down at the clipboard in front of her. I watched as Shade swallowed hard and then hurried out of the backroom into the front of the house.

"I was trying to figure out how many of the vanilla creamers you want me to order. I couldn't find the normal ordering rate on the sheet," she said, glancing up at me. "You okay?"

My eyes shifted to hers, and I scowled. "You have the worst timing ever. You are like this fae pro at sensing people's emotions, but you have no idea when you're about to interrupt something."

I threw my hands up in the air and headed toward the door. Willa was staring at me, confused. "Does that mean I order several boxes? I feel like I missed something here."

As I pushed through into the front of the house, I chuckled, hearing her running behind me. Now that I knew she was a fae, the little things I assumed were absentmindedness before suddenly became clear. She wasn't human and didn't thoroughly pick up on the social cues. It was funny, but not that funny. I just hoped that wouldn't be the only chance I ever had to have a moment with Shade. I had no idea how he felt about me, but I was starting to get a good idea of how I felt for him.

6

Callie

"Because I said so," I growled, staring at Mr. Hobbles as he stood on the countertop, pacing back and forth.

"So, you're telling me that not only are you leaving me here with Bean and his tiny brain, but you're also leaving me here with two perfect strangers," Hobbles replied. "Meanwhile, you're off gallivanting in some other plane of existence, with no idea when you'll come home. That's *if* you even come home."

I spun on my heels and pointed at Hobbles,

having a hard time being angry when I was staring at a cat. "Don't say that. Of course, I'm going to come home. I told you, I'm going to the fae realm to help Willa find her father and figure out who took the stone. Esmeralda and Harry are trusted members of the fae community, and I need somebody to stay behind and watch the shop. Bella and Cruz are doing me a favor by staying here so you don't miss a meal. Don't make me put you in one of those cat hotels."

He gasped. "That's the second time you threatened me with that, and I don't appreciate it. I can already feel the fleas crawling on me. I just don't understand why I can't come with you. It's a travesty to leave me here with the mutt."

I let out an exhaustive sigh and patted him on the top of his head. "I know you love him, even if you won't admit it. We're family. He's not that bad."

Just then, Bean went running past the kitchen door, tripping over his own ear and sliding past on his face. Mr. Hobbles turned toward me, but I shook my head and put up my hand. "We can't all be as graceful as you. Besides, I absolutely can't take you to the fae realm. The last thing I need is to be worrying about my life while I'm cleaning up your trail of kitty litter paw prints down some castle hallway."

Hobbles sat down and licked his paw indignantly. "It's not my fault you buy the cheap litter. If you spring for the automatic cleaner and the crystals, you'll never have to worry about it."

I groaned, turning toward the cabinet and reaching up, grabbing a tumbler and filling it with coffee. I spooned some sugar into the cup and poured a little cream before stirring it and twisting the top back on. Willa walked into the kitchen, shooting a bitter look toward the cat. As soon as she looked at me, though, her mouth turned upward into a smile. "You ready to go?"

I put out my hands. "As ready as I'll ever be. You told me not to bring anything, and I actually slept last night. Don't think I don't know that you and Shade used magic on me for sleep. I was dreaming about cotton candy and yoga pants. You could've at least given me an interesting dream."

Willa's cheeks went red, and she smirked. "Haven't you had enough interesting dreams lately? We just thought it would be good for you to get a good night's sleep before we go to the fae realm tonight."

I took a sip of my coffee and shrugged. In reality, I really appreciated the ability to sleep through the night. Still, I didn't like it when they used magic on me without telling me first. I knew I could be stubborn, but it just felt wrong in some way. "What are you doing? Are you ready?"

Willa rolled her eyes. "Ready? To go back to a place that I escaped long ago to have a normal life? To go back home and suddenly become the queen, which was against everything I ever wanted to do? And on top of that, have to find the King Collector and whoever stole the stone? Oh sure, I'm bursting at the seams in anticipation."

I snickered, choking on my coffee. "I'll be there with you."

"Me too," Shade said, walking into the kitchen behind Willa.

Hobbles rolled his eyes. "What a happy little family…."

Willa chuckled at him as he jumped down and ran off into the living room. Shade made his way over to the coffee cups and poured himself a cup, glancing over at Willa with a raised eyebrow. She shook her head and turned back to me. "Want to watch one last movie or something?"

I glanced over at the clock on the microwave and shook my head. "In all honesty? I want to go over to the cemetery where my parents are buried just in case I don't get to come back for a while."

"I'll go with you," Shade said, wrinkling his nose at the bitterness of the coffee. "You shouldn't really be going out by yourself."

I glanced over at Willa, who looked like she wanted to agree with him, but she knew I'd kill her. I smiled at Shade and took another sip of my drink, leaving my eyes watching him. "No offense toward you at all, but I know that you guys want to protect me everywhere I go, and this is something I do by myself."

Willa nodded. "It's true. In all the years that we've been best friends, the only time I've ever been with her to the cemetery was..."

It was the funeral. She had come to the funeral. We never talked about it, though, and even standing there in the kitchen, nonchalantly discussing it, she couldn't bring herself to say the words. The one person who had seen me grow and move out of my mourning was Willa. The person I was back then when my parents had died and the person I was that day standing in the kitchen were two different people.

I braced myself for Shade's argument, but surprisingly, he didn't even attempt it. Instead, he set his coffee cup down and rubbed his hands together before stepping forward and hovering them just inches from my face. He closed his eyes and began to whisper. His words were quiet and not anything I could understand. Small silk-like waves of magic came from his hands and swirled around me, over my head, my shoulders, down my sides, and all the way down to the bottom of my feet. I stood very still, surprising myself with the idea that I actually fully trusted him. He didn't need to tell me that he was putting a protection spell on me. I already knew that.

When he was done, the magic drifted into my skin and disappeared from view. He gave me a once-over, and I couldn't tell whether he was checking me out or just making sure that the magic had covered all of me. Maybe it was a little bit of both. I grabbed my keys and purse and walked toward the kitchen door, pausing and turning back toward Willa. "I'll be back soon. I won't be there that long."

Willa nodded. "Just make sure you have your cell phone on you. And if you feel like anybody is watching you or following you, call us. Don't hesitate. We're really close to getting to the fae world, and one thing I do have to say about that is you will be under my protection. As queen regent, that means you'll have an army protecting you. But here, there's not much I can do."

I smiled at Willa, shifting my eyes to Shade, and then headed out, hopping into my SUV. I turned on the music low in the car and shook the anxiety from my shoulders as I made the drive over to the cemetery. It wasn't that long of a trip. It was right out of town, up on top of a hill that overlooked the ocean. It was the perfect place, exactly what my mother would've wanted, and I wasn't even the one who had picked it out.

Growing up, I had never really pictured my parents as planners when it came to death, but shockingly enough, after they had passed away, I found they had made all the necessary plans. I didn't even have to pick a headstone, lift a hand, or pay for anything for that matter. Everything had been taken care of. Sometimes it comforted me, thinking that perhaps they did all of that because they always wanted to make sure that I was taken care of. Even in death, they took care of me like they had in life.

On the other hand, it always bothered me a little bit. It wasn't like my parents had dangerous jobs or risky hobbies. It seems strange that two people in their forties had their entire funeral planned out, down to what food was served at the wake.

As I drove slowly down the winding path, through the cemetery, and up the hill, I glanced out at the bunches of flowers peppering the gravestones. My parent's plots were private, sitting on top of the hill with its own parking space and a picket fence that surrounded the entire top of the mound. I hadn't been there in a long time. I had come to the cemetery, but I hadn't actually climbed the hill for a couple of years. It was hard for me to face their names on the stones.

Stepping out of the car, I first looked out at the ocean in the distance, taking in the salty sea air that blew around me. I grabbed the light jacket from the backseat and popped the collar, feeling the bite of the wind off the ocean. As I turned, I stopped in my tracks, staring at the statue that had been placed before I arrived at the cemetery to bury my parents. I had always thought it was a beautiful statue, and in my mind, I had remembered it as an angel. But standing there in front of it that day, after everything I had been through, I realized it wasn't an angel at all.

The statue was of a woman standing and staring out toward the ocean. She had long hair, and her dress was light and flowing, blowing behind her. She was barefoot, and she had wings coming from her back. I guess after all the years and all the trips there, my mind just automatically assumed she had been an angel. But those wings weren't feathered, and there was no halo. Instead, as the sun hit the statue's face, it sparkled and shimmered. Within the stone were tiny specks of glittering material. The wings were like those of a butterfly, only folded toward her back.

Walking toward the statue, I looked up at her face, realizing just how giant the figure was. At her feet was a small, engraved sign with both my mother's and my father's name on it. I ran my hand over the top of it, wiping away the mud and dirt that had collected from storms over the years. That was when I felt it. There was more engraved beneath their names, but it was too small to really read from where I was standing. I squatted down and ran my fingers over the engraving, but my forty-year-old eyes couldn't make out what it said. I patted my pockets, wondering if I had a piece of paper and maybe a pencil to trace over it, but I didn't keep things like that in my pockets.

So, I made a mental note of it and figured I'd come back after returning from the fae realm and figure out exactly what it said. It was probably one of my mom's favorite lines from a book, or my father's hilarious dad jokes that he used to tell all the time. It was a little Easter egg that they knew would take me a little while to find. They'd always been good with things like that. They would make me remember things that had long since been tucked away in the drawers of my mind.

Standing up, I smoothed out my shirt and walked over to the two headstones side by side. I tilted my head and took a long deep breath, feeling that twinge in my heart seeing their names engraved in stone. "Hey, guys. I know, it's been a while. I guess I've struggled through the years. I used to come here all the time and talk to you both. My therapist told me I came here an unhealthy number of times, so I stopped seeing him. But I guess, in a way, he was right. When I should've been out moving forward with my life, I was sitting here talking to two stone engravings as if you were really still here with me."

I walked around the graves to a small bench that sat right next to them. That was my addition to the area. It was a place I could sit and talk to them without having to pull out a blanket or sit on the ground. It was a place I could take in the sea air if I wanted to or tell my parents what I'd been up to.

"So, things have been a bit crazy. The coffee shop is doing really well, and Willa has no idea what she's doing, but it always seems to work out. So, I found out that magic is real and my best friend is a fae, and the guy I have a crush on is a real-life witch. Oh, and there's a whole other realm of beings. There could be multiple realms of beings. I'm not really sure at this point. It's kind of confusing."

I went on and on, letting it all out, telling them about the adventure that I had been on and what I had coming up. It felt so good to talk to my mom and dad, and the sadness that I usually had when I went there wasn't nearly as bad as before. There was a strength inside me, something I didn't notice until I stood on that hilltop, talking to my parents.

"Anyway, so that's why I'm here. I'm leaving in a few hours to go to this fae realm, and I'm not exactly sure when I'll be back. But don't worry about me. I promise I can handle this. I love you, guys, and I miss you a lot. I'll come to visit as soon as I get back."

I put my hands on my knees and stood up, staring down at their headstones one last time. A warm puff of air trickled down my neck, and my body stiffened. At first, I thought it was just a rogue blast of heat mixed in with the cool air coming off the ocean, but it was accompanied by a low grunt when it happened again. Slowly I turned around, finding myself face to face with an enormously large chest covered in denim overalls. I tilted my head upward, craning to see the face in front of me.

The man was a tall brute with long brown hair and a large square chin. His forehead was wide and dipped down over his brow. His face was expressionless as he stood there, staring at me. The protection spell around me shimmered from my head to my toes, and I slowly began to take a step backward. However, before I could make a break for it, he reached his enormous hand out and grabbed my arm.

A flash of heat rolled over me, and the protection spell began to fracture, breaking into small pieces and crumbling to the ground around me. The magic seeped into the soil as the man tightened his grip and grunted once again.

My heart sank, and I shook my head. "Great. Not again."

7

Shade

THE SOUND of my footsteps echoed through Callie's quiet house as I slowly paced forward and back in front of the fireplace.

I glanced down at the ashes in the bottom and wondered how long it had been since she had actually had a fire in there. Of course, that wasn't my main thought.

My main thought was centered around where in the world Callie was. She said she would be quick, but it had been hours since she had left to go to the cemetery. Callie was a lot of things, she had an adventurous spirit, but she was also cautious and thoughtful. With everything going on, I had a hard time believing she would just decide to be gone for hours and not let us know.

I glanced over at Willa as she clicked off her phone and set it on the seat next to her.

She leaned back into the cushion on the couch. "She didn't answer. Actually, it went right to voicemail, but she's really terrible at charging her phone. I'm sure she just lost track of time talking with her parents and maybe stopped to get a cup of coffee or something."

I breathed deeply, trying to sense the protection spell that I had put around her. Nothing seemed off, but my senses in that town were a little less potent than they were back home. Stopping and looking over at the pictures on her fireplace mantel, I picked one up. "Are these her parents?"

Willa forced a smile. "Yeah. They were in a horrible accident when we were in our first year of college, and both died. Callie has taken it really hard all these years. It's been a lot of years, but for her, it feels like yesterday. She's progressed, though."

I smiled at the young version of Callie in the picture and then set it back onto the mantle.

Shoving my hands into my pockets, I continued to pace but slowed myself down a bit. "The fae realm is magnificent, though I wish this wasn't the reason we were going."

"But would you actually be going to the fae realm if this weren't the reason?"

"No, probably not," I replied with a short chuckle. "My brother's always needed constant tending to. It's not like he's helpless, but he's not a ruthless leader. I think you know as well as I do that being a king or queen requires a certain level of..."

"Dishonesty?" she asked.

I lifted a brow. "I was thinking more along the lines of courage and the ability to separate your emotions from your duty. But I guess, in a way, dishonesty is part of it as well."

Willa let out a deep sigh. "Well, it sounds like your brother and I have a lot in common. I'm not the kind of ruler my father was or my grandfather. They weren't bad, but they were everything you would think of when you thought of the fae royal line. I took after my mother. I knew that I wasn't cut out for it, and I knew if I stayed, I'd end up like her. So, I left."

I wasn't sure what to say to that, but I knew I had to say something. I could see her looking for my initial response. I could only imagine the kind of anger or judgmental responses she had gotten in the past. "I don't blame you one bit. I was never even thought of to be the king. Not unless something happened to my brother. So, I wasn't groomed for it, and I never prepared myself for it. Had I been born knowing my whole life that I would one day be king? I might've made the same decision as you. I may be a serious leader, but I'm not a king, either. I don't possess the kind heart that my brother has. I think to be a well-rounded king, I would need all of it. My father was that kind of king."

Willa smiled. "I remember your father. He was fun to be around when he came to visit. I remember you as well when you were a child."

I winced, thinking about myself as a lanky, skinny child. "Right before my brother became king, you were already gone. I think you had just left because things were cautious in the fae realm at that point. It had been many years since I had been there, and it was strange to me how differently I saw everything with adult eyes compared to children's."

Willa nodded, her eyes steady on mine. "I know what happened that time. I still had connections with the fae realm at first, and they let me know. They were worried about my safety, but they weren't after me. My father still thinks it was someone on the Council, but he could never figure it out. It wouldn't have shocked me. Not all of the Council agreed with the alliance or truce that we have with the witches. Some of them harbor some very deep-rooted hatred. But as time passes, the elders will move on, and many have been replaced by younger fae. Fae who grew up in a world where the truce and alliance were there, hearing only stories from a long time ago when we were enemies."

"I think perhaps the witches harbor a bit more anger toward the fae and have held on to that through many generations, but my brother is very dedicated to stopping that. To changing minds. I'm proud of him."

Willa started to say something, but her words quickly faded away, and I found myself reaching up and grabbing onto the mantle to stabilize me. A shocking jolt of energy reverberated through my entire being, my vision crisscrossing, and everything became a blur around me. There were flashes of images in my mind, but the only one I could make out was my magic crumbling into tiny shards and dropping to the ground.

"Shade?" I could hear Willa calling me.

I squeezed my eyes tightly shut and pushed the echoing magical force from my body. When the ground felt solid beneath me, I took a deep breath. I opened my eyes, staring directly at Willa, who looked extremely worried.

"The protection spell... Somebody broke it."

"What?" Willa gasped. "This is the second time, maybe even more, that a being has broken the spell by a mighty being. Where are they coming from? Who are these people?"

I released my grip on the mantle and put my hands onto my knees, taking long deep breaths to clear away the rest of the reactionary magic pulsing in my head. "I don't know, but I do know that Callie's in trouble."

Willa clenched her teeth and began to pace back and forth in front of me. "We should've put tracking on her. I thought about it, but I didn't do it because I felt bad. I didn't want her to think we were babysitting her."

Carefully, I stood back up and rolled my shoulders, rubbing my hands together. "Well, that only makes one of us. I put a tracking spell on her. I figured she could get as mad as she wanted to, but at least I would know that she was safe."

Willa's eyes went wide, and she stepped back as I began to work my magic, twisting and turning it within my palms. When I felt the energy at its peak, I opened my hands. A large bubble floated upward and hovered between the two of us. Within the bubble, we could see images, like a movie playing out in front of us.

I squinted, trying to make out what was in the image. It was fuzzy at first but slowly began to clear. Willa tilted her head to the side. "Is this from her perspective?"

I nodded. "Yeah, and it looks like she's waking up from whatever magic was put on her. Is that the back of someone's legs?"

No sooner had I asked the question, the viewpoint of the video moved upward, and it seemed that Callie was waking up, looking around. The ground beneath them was cement with large cracks running through it and tall weeds growing from the cracks. She turned to one side, and I could see a rusting metal wall with graffiti painted on it. She turned to the left, and there was another, that one darker in color.

The bouncing steps of whoever was carrying her stopped, and she was set down onto her feet. For a moment, she stared straight at the broad chest of someone I couldn't make out, and then she turned toward the door.

Willa gasped. "I know where that is. That's the

warehouse district. There's a bunch of abandoned warehouses there that aren't used anymore. They were flooded years ago from the storm."

Callie's vision bounced back and forth, and the last thing we saw before the tracking cut out was the number 127 on a large metal door that led into a warehouse. The bubble popped in front of us. Willa shook her head angrily. "Dammit. We've got to hurry. We gotta save Callie, and we only have six hours until the portal opens. After that, who knows when the next time we'll be able to go through. Even worse, who knows, the next time someone will be able to come here to help us."

Willa was right.

The magic I was experiencing and seeing was far more robust than anything I'd witnessed before. If we missed our portal, I wasn't sure that we could protect ourselves from what was coming after Callie.

8

Callie

THE BIG BRUTE sat me down on my feet, and I wobbled back and forth for a moment as all the blood came flowing back through my body.

It felt like I had been drugged, even though I hadn't. Try being slung over somebody's shoulder and bouncing up and down for twenty minutes as he slowly makes his way to wherever the hell we were. Before I could fully see around me, though, he pushed me forward, opening up a large metal door with a number 127 on the front of it, almost completely faded off.

Every few feet, he would shove me forward, and it was dark, but there were no obstacles in my way. As my eyes adjusted, I realized I was in the center of a vast, empty warehouse. The concrete floors were stained with whatever had been there. The stench of old car oil and grease radiated from them. In the very center of the room was a chair. I looked up at the big brute and back at the chair. "I'm assuming that's for me?"

He gave a long nod and grabbed both of my hands, tying a heavy, scratchy rope around my wrists. When he was done knotting it about ten times, he turned me and pressed hard, forcing my legs to collapse as I sat down in the chair. His heavy hand stayed gripped to my shoulder, pushing downward to ensure that I wasn't going to get up and run away. That was smart. It was actually the first thing I had planned to do. However, his strength was far more significant than mine, so I growled at him but stayed seated.

"What show is this? I've always wanted to see *Cats*." I snickered to myself, but the large man didn't even flinch, looking forward into the shadows.

"I'm afraid that show was canceled long ago," a voice said from those same shadows. "Though I did see it when it first came out, and it was amazing."

"Who's there?" I yelled out. "Show yourself. Time is ticking, and I don't really have a lot of it."

The brazenness that I was showing almost shocked me. Granted, even with the King Collector, I didn't really bite my tongue, but it appeared that I had grown a bit more courageous since Rome. With courage came sarcasm. I knew that was probably not the best way to handle being abducted but come on. How many times?

The tapping of footsteps drew my attention to the right-hand corner of the building. I squinted, looking through the dark as a figure emerged. At first, all I could see was the shimmer reflecting off of his shoes and cane, tap, tap, tapping as he walked. I braced myself for what I was about to see, knowing that what I'd seen in the past was terrifying. However, as the figure emerged into the light, I couldn't hold back a chuckle.

The man was tall and thin, wearing a dusty top hat. He had a cape tied over his shoulders, but it was short, stopping only halfway down his back. As the cape fluttered, I could see he was wearing a vest, button-up white shirt, and dress pants. He reached up and took off his hat, holding it to his chest. He bent forward in a bow. He had jet-black hair that was slicked back like a magician. He looked like he belonged in a different century. He held the top of an intricately carved cane with silver accents swirling around in his gloved right hand.

I lifted a brow. "What the hell are you supposed to be? I asked for *Cats*, and I got a low-budget version of *The Phantom of the Opera*."

The man's eyes shifted up toward mine, but he didn't frown. In fact, he had the opposite reaction completely. A smile curved on his lips, and he began to laugh as he stood up and put his hat back on. "You're funny. I think I half expected that since your mother was funny."

Immediately my face hardened, and I gripped my fists tighter. "What do you know about my parents?"

He looked at me curiously for a second and then around the building, putting his arms dramatically out to each side as if he were announcing a circus in the 1940s. "I want to apologize for the whole dramatic scene. This usually isn't my kind of thing, but I needed to get you here quickly and without anyone following you. This warehouse district is a maze of buildings, so even if someone were tracking you, it'd take a bit for them to get here."

"But they will get here," I replied. "And when they do..."

The man tilted his head back and laughed. "I expect I'll be in for it. We should probably get on with this before they show up."

A spark of fear ran through me, unsure of what he meant by getting on with things. Was I brought there as a sacrifice? Did the King Collector hire someone new to take me down? If they did, my bracelet wasn't even attempting to protect me at that point. I felt no energy or magic running through it. I clenched my teeth, pulling the fear back away from me, knowing that it wouldn't help anything. I lifted my chin and squared my shoulders. "What the hell are you supposed to be? The robe figure with red, beady eyes had a lot more effectiveness."

"Oh, where are my manners? My name is Alabaster, and I'm very much like your friends. Though I'm not a witch or a fae, I am from the fae realm."

Immediately my eyes narrowed, my heart beating faster in my chest. Had someone opened the portal early? "Did..."

He was already shaking his head. "Did the queen regent send me? No. I wasn't sent by anyone. I've been here for a very long time."

I was starting to get confused. "Okay, then what the hell do you want for me? I'm not a fae or a witch. And I have nothing to offer you."

He smiled, walking closer to me. I blinked several times, finding myself staring into a set of very familiar green eyes. It was so strange. His eyes were so similar to my mother's. My mother always had striking eyes; their color was slightly different from most people with green eyes. They were vibrant and something she always got compliments on.

He came closer and bent over, looking at my face as if he were committing it to memory. "I want you to take me with you to the fae world. Your portal opens soon, and I want to come with you."

I pulled my brows together, stared at him for a second, and then burst into laughter. He stood up and shook his head, holding his cane under his arm as he removed his gloves. For a second there, I thought maybe, just maybe, he was related to my mother, but he was just another enemy in the fae saga I was living.

"Why in the world would I take you with me to the fae realm? You may be from there, but it's obvious that you haven't been back in a very long time."

He shrugged, putting his gloves into his pocket, bringing his cane back down to the ground. "I'm from there, but you're right. I haven't been there in many years. In fact, it's been a few hundred years since I've been to the fae realm. I came through the portal chasing love, and then I got stuck here. It turns out she wasn't quite the woman I thought she was."

I blinked at him. "It happens to the best of us. But right now, it is not the time, nor am I the person who needs to be asked if you can go back to the fae realm. If you're from the fae world, then contact them with your magic or however it works. I can't help you."

He gave me a half-smile and looked up at his bodyguard. "She really hasn't learned much about the fae realm, has she?"

I looked up at the big guy, but he didn't reply. "Do you make it a habit of keeping gigantic, brainless oafs around to do your dirty work?"

Again, Alabaster chuckled. "I can help you find the fae king and the witch king. I have certain gifts that most others do not."

Immediately, my face went straight, and my heart pattered faster in my chest. I narrowed my eyes and gritted my teeth. "How did you know about that? How do you know who I am? How do you know who I am enough to know that I'd be at the cemetery?"

"Well, my dear, that's pretty simple." He kicked the bottom of his cane and flipped it up under his arm as he came forward and squatted at eye level with me. "I'm your uncle."

Oh shit.

9

Callie

THE BRUTE LIFTED his hand from my shoulder, and I quickly popped to my feet.

Everything in my head screamed to turn and run, but I knew that was stupid. The guy wasn't going to let me just run out of there. I was absolutely livid.

It was one thing to kidnap somebody and try to save them for your collection, but it was another for him to use my parents against me like that. That was a different kind of cruel.

"You're full of shit. Both of my parents were

only children. They never once talked about having any siblings. Nor did my grandmother or grandfather talk about having any other children. If you think that talking about my dead family will rattle me, you've got another thing coming. They've been dead a long time."

I looked the man up and down. Part of me tried to remember everything about him so that if I got out of there, I'd be able to tell Willa. The other part of me, a very small portion, was looking for any kind of similarities between him and my mother beyond the eyes. He was a strange man and reminded me of a cross between the Johnny Depp version of Willy Wonka and Doc from back to the future.

He stepped back several paces and clutched his hands in front of him, keeping a calm smile on his face. I glanced over at the big guy and knew that he may be slow, but he would be hard to get around. I focused on the bracelet around my wrist, praying that it would send some sort of energy or magic my way, but it wasn't doing anything.

"I know it's hard to believe, but I'm your mother's older brother. She didn't talk about me because, well, she never met me."

I shook my head, trying to put it together.

"But you said you're from the fae realm. We aren't magical people. I just happen to have a best friend who's the fae princess. It's completely coincidental."

He smirked at me, and it gave me a strange feeling. "You're right. You are not magical people. Your mother and I shared a mom, but our fathers were not the same. My father was from the fae realm, but I doubt your grandmother even knew that. She was very young, and it was both of their first loves."

My brow wrinkled. "But if my grandmother had another child, why would she never talk about you?"

He tilted his head from right to left. "It's complicated. I'll be honest with you, I don't fully know the answer to that, but I have my suspicions. I belonged in the fae realm, and my father knew that. He knew I couldn't grow up here in this one, nor could he stay in this one. My father died many, many years ago, and he rarely ever talked about my mother. I can only assume he used some sort of spell on her to get rid of her memory. He couldn't take her with him to the fae realm, but he also loved her so much he wouldn't have left her hurting."

I shook my head in disbelief. "So what you're

telling me is this really is a crazy case of coincidence?"

He pointed at me with a grin. "I've been wondering that same exact thing. I don't have an answer for you. But, if you take me to the fae realm with you, I might be able to find those answers. My... abilities are stifled here in this realm."

I stared at him, not saying a word. It was a struggle, wanting to believe that I had a family member, someone related to me somehow, so I wasn't the only one left. Sometimes it got really lonely not having any family. At the same time, I didn't trust him in the least. From an outside perspective, I knew I shouldn't believe a word he was saying.

"What powers do you have? If you're not a fae or witch, then what creature are you?"

He winced, dramatically placing his hand over his heart. "Creature? I'm not a creature. And I can see that you're struggling with all of this. You want to believe that I'm your uncle, but you don't trust me."

I lifted my bound wrists and glanced over at the bodyguard. "You haven't exactly given me any reason to trust you. The last time that I checked, one didn't really kidnap family. Instead, people usually give them a call on the phone and then meet up at a family reunion."

"That wouldn't be much of a family reunion for you, would it? You're the only one left, well, except for me. We are very different, though. The day after I was born, I was taken back to the fae realm. I..."

My handler grunted, and Alabaster stopped, lifting a brow. "What's that, Tiny?"

I rolled my eyes. "Really? His name is Tiny?"

Alabaster pulled out the pocket watch from the small pocket on his vest and flipped it open. "Ah, thank you, old friend. The time is ticking by pretty fast." His attention turned back to me. "As much as I'd love to tell you all about where I came from and connect the dots that I know are driving you crazy in your head right now, I will have to take a rain check. I need you to take me to speak to Princess Willa if you will. I'll explain everything to her and your witch friend and let the chips fall where they may. And then, if they allow me back into the fae realm, you and I can have a proper conversation over a cup of coffee."

I looked at him and then up at the big man, watching as he slowly turned toward me, his head never swiveling on his massive neck. He grumbled as he looked down at me, and I was starting to think that whatever he was grumbling was his own type of language. Alabaster seemed to understand him. He reached out and put his hand on my shoulder, and I could feel the heaviness weighing me down.

Turning back to Alabaster, I let out a deep sigh. "This isn't a request, is it?"

Alabaster put his gloves back on and smiled at me. "I'm afraid it's not. I need to speak to the princess, and I need to do it before you leave."

"Then speak," a voice said from behind us.

Alabaster's eyes went wide, and he looked up at the same time as I spun around. Stepping into the flickering lights, Willa stood like a superhero with her hands on her hips right next to Shade, who already had magic forming in his palms.

I turned back to my supposed uncle and smiled. "Well, here you are. I doubt, though, that they'll listen to anything you have to say. Next time, maybe try that cup of coffee from the beginning."

Just then, Shade swayed his arms back and forth and pressed his palms outward from his chest. From the palms of his hands shot a single bolt of magical lightning. First, it hit the big guy, knocking him from his feet. However, it didn't stop there. It ricocheted off of him and hit the

SOME LIKE IT HEXED

ground, sending a barrage of smaller magical bolts bouncing off of each other, striking the ground all around Alabaster.

Willa waved to me, and I looked over at the big guy before taking off and running straight over to them. When I reached them, I turned quickly, expecting to see the man chasing after me, but that wasn't what happened. Instead, he stood, his cane on the ground, scrunched into a ball with his hands up in the air. The lightning crackled and struck around him for several moments until finally, it dissipated. Willa crossed her arms over her chest. "What did you want with Callie?"

"Careful," I whispered. "That's definitely a loaded question."

Alabaster didn't answer.

Willa looked over at Shade and shrugged her shoulders. "It seems he needs a little more to loosen up those nerves."

Shade pushed up his sleeves and grinned, putting his hands together. "It would be my pleasure. I could take a little off the top, you know, give him a little bit of motivation."

It was comical to see Willa and Shade interacting how they were like they were partners in crime. It seemed that my time away from them was good, helping them to form a better bond. Neither one of them liked to admit it, but I knew it would take all hands to find the kings and recover the stone.

Suddenly, Alabaster's voice cracked, his tone several octaves higher than when he had talked to me. He took one glove off and carefully waved it over his head, still scrunched into a ball with black marks all around him on the ground. "No need. There's no need. I can explain everything. I have something that can help you."

"Why would we need your help with anything? We don't even know who you are," Willa replied.

She quietly shook her head at Shade, knowing she had the guy talking. He looked almost disappointed, and it made me smirk, but I put my head down to hide it. Willa took a couple steps forward, staring at Alabaster.

"Well?"

Alabaster lifted his head and looked around. "I'm just going to throw you a vision orb, okay?"

Both Shade and Willa narrowed their eyes, looking back at each other. It seemed they realized that he may be telling the truth, at least when it came to having something to help them. Willa shrugged and gave him a nod, stepping back next to Shade and me. Shade moved his hands again, creating a barrier between him and us, just in case. It shimmered purple like his protection spell had on me.

Alabaster finally stood up, picking up his hat from the ground and setting it carefully on his head. He brushed off his clothes and straightened his jacket, twisting the tie of his cape back around to the front of his neck. He closed his eyes and began to hum, lifting his hand and curling his fingers into the shape of an O. He gently blew into the hole like blowing bubbles as a child, his hand acting as the wand. My eyes went wider as I watched the magical orb grow larger and larger before disconnecting from his fingers and floating through the air. It stopped in front of the three of us, and a vision began to clear within it. Shade pulled his magic back into him, all three of us stepping forward to watch what was happening inside the orb. The vision was fuzzy, but it was obvious who it was.

"Father?" Willa gasped.

Looking at the image within the orb, I recognized that face from pictures Willa had around her house. He looked battered, the blueness of his eyes fading to gray. The vision was only a second, maybe even less than that, but it was enough to get Willa's attention. Alabaster pulled the orb back into his hand and squeezed his hand shut tightly around it before opening it again and watching tiny specks of magic fall from his palms.

Shade shook his head, looking over at Willa and me and then back at Alabaster. Willa narrowed her eyes as if she knew what Shade was thinking, but I had no idea what was going on. He said he wasn't a fae, yet he could use magic. I didn't know the rules or the ins and outs of different beings. I didn't know how many magical people there were out there. But one thing was evident, Alabaster wasn't joking about being part of the fae community.

Shade put up his hand. "You're... You're a finder." His face was riddled with confusion. "But finder haven't been seen in over two thousand years."

Alabaster perked up and slowly nodded, bringing himself back to his feet. "That's right. I'm the last finder, and I'm the only one who can help you find your father and your brother."

10

Callie

I STOOD BESIDE WILLA, and we both watched as Shade ambled in circles around Alabaster.

His hands moved up and down, his eyes closed, and everything was silent. He stayed that way, using his magic to detect any manipulation Alabaster may be using.

"Finders are powerful, but they don't have strong enough magic to manipulate someone. That's not usually magic that's allowed, but those who do practice are usually witches or fae, or even warlocks."

I lifted my brow at Willa as she watched, her eyes not leaving Alabaster for even a second. She was right not to trust, and neither did I, but I was definitely curious. When Shade was finally done, he stepped back from the finder and joined Willa and me.

Alabaster smiled and put out his hands. "What do you say? Did I pass the test?"

Shade looked at him suspiciously and then turned to Willa and me. "He's actually a finder. There's no manipulation from him, and he's not hiding anything. Beyond his annoyingly happy personality and yet another addition of sarcasm to our team, he seems to be telling the truth."

I closed my eyes for a second shook my head. "Okay, putting the whole he's my uncle thing to the side, what the hell is a finder?"

Willa bit the inside of her cheek, taking a moment to think about her response. "Finders haven't really been around for a very long time, but from what I know of them, they do just that, they watch. They can see anything, in any realm, at any time, past, present, or future. They can look through their crystal ball of sorts, but they can't directly give someone the answer to what they're looking for."

I puffed out my cheeks, looking from Willa to

Shade and back again. "So, what's the point if they can't give you the answer?"

"They have to pose the answer in the form of clues or riddles." Willa rolled her eyes. "They were used as the main force behind the guard for centuries. But, since they can't really protect themselves with magic, they were easily killed off. They became the most hunted form of magical being in all the realms."

The three of us looked over at him as he stood there, brushing his bodyguard off and doing the same to the front of his suit. He looked so strange, and the whole idea of him was weird. "So he could technically help us find the two kings and the stone."

Shade opened his mouth, but he closed it quickly again. He stood there contemplative for a moment before dramatically shaking his head. He seemed curious, but he quickly turned from the idea. From the moment he realized that Alabaster was a finder, he became skeptical and nervous. But if finders hadn't been around for two thousand years, then I wasn't sure how Shade would've had the opportunity to meet one, much less be incredibly suspicious of them. For all intents and purposes, the one standing before us didn't really seem that intimidating.

Shaking his head, Shade crossed his arms over his chest. "Sure, they may be able to post the answers in the form of riddles and questions, but half the time, they'll send you on a wild goose chase. It's only after you've gone on this chase that you realize it wasn't the answer you needed to narrow down the field. Finders were notorious for having people search for the rest of their lives and never find the answers they're looking for. Finders have turned people crazy. They've used magical beings, mixing their watching abilities with the magical one's intuition and detective skills. But as soon as they figure out where the treasure, or the person, or the secret is, they throw in a confusing question or riddle to send the person off the trail so they can reap the benefits of finding."

Willa looked at her watch. "The problem is, we don't have time to figure out what this guy's reasoning for getting back to the fae world is. At the same time, he showed me my father, which means that he can help us find them."

"But we don't know that for sure," Shade replied. "What he showed you was a limit of what he's allowed to show you as a finder. There are rules to it, though. Whatever he showed you could've been from a month ago. Hell, it could've been from ten years ago. You just don't realize it."

"But if you leave me here, you'll never know at all," the finder said, smiling in our direction. "With the current state of affairs of the magical community, my cover has been blown. It's time for me to go back under the protection of the fae. If you leave me here, I will die, and there won't be another finder to help you find your father and your brother." His eyes shifted to mine. "And you'll be leaving behind your only living relative."

I shook my head. "Whether that's the truth or not remains to be seen, but I'm not the one who makes this decision. That's Willa, your future queen."

"Queen regent," Willa whispered, rolling her eyes. "I do not want the job for the rest of my time. But, the finder's right. If he really can help us find my father and your brother, he's the best we've come up with so far, and we won't have a chance to come back and get him if we leave him here."

I could see on Shade's face that he wasn't happy with that decision, but I could also see that he knew it wasn't his choice. It wasn't his world, and he wasn't the one who would be making the decisions. Willa walked toward Alabaster, her shoulders back, a different air to her. She was more confident, graceful. She was starting to look more and more like the queen every day. "I'll let you come with us. But, you have to stay at the castle, and you have to attempt to help find what we're looking for. If you do those things, I'll let you stay in the fae world."

Alabaster took off his hat and crossed his arm over his stomach, bowing deeply to her. "Thank you for your grace, Your Majesty."

I pressed my lips together, trying not to laugh at the sound of that. Willa already knew and had snapped her head back, looking at me, a smirk across her lips. "Don't you do it. You're going to hear that a lot when we cross realms."

I stood up straight, bent one leg back, and pretended to lift a skirt as I curtsied to her. "Your Grace."

Alabaster laughed, and Willa rolled her eyes, walking back over toward us. "Great, another sarcastic person. You guys are going to be the death of me."

The alarm on Willa's watch started to beep, and she looked down, her eyes growing wide. "Shit, we've got to go. We're like five miles from the pier. There's no way we can make it there on foot."

Shade walked forward and put out his hand. "It's a short transport. It won't be too bad."

My stomach was already turning from the thought of it, but I knew we had no other choice. There was no way that we could make it five miles in the next ten minutes. We all gathered around together, including Alabaster and his bodyguard. One by one, we touched hands until we were all connected. Shade glanced over at me and then did his thing, transporting us from the warehouses to the pier. My body felt like it was being tossed back and forth, my stomach flip-flopping, everything spinning in circles around me until finally, my feet found the old creaky boards of the pier.

As soon as we released hands, a wild burst of energy began to race up and down my arm, from my bracelet to my shoulder. Rays of magic, golden in color, spiraled around me and the four others stepped back, watching me with wide eyes.

I looked over at Willa, slightly frightened. "What's going on?"

"My aunt, she used the bracelet as a key to the portal. All you can do is stand there at this point."

That was easier said than done. As the golden rays began to shoot from the bracelet, my arm lifted into the air. The scene in front of us began to crack, a portal ripping in midair. It was hard for my brain to comprehend what I was seeing. The energy pumped from me over and over again, spiking at the portal until it grew large enough for all of us to step through. Willa went first, then Alabaster and his bodyguard. Running down the pier, Harry and Esmerelda had bags packed and smiles on their faces. They grinned at me as they passed, jumping headfirst through the portal.

"I want you to go ahead of me," Shade said. "I just want to make sure you get through okay."

I looked back at my world, the beautiful ocean, the houses with all the lights on, and the beaches that stretched for miles and miles. I took a deep breath and hoped that it wasn't the last time I would see it. Either way, I had to move forward because there was no going back at that point. The fae realm beckoned, and like it or not, I had to answer the call.

Callie

"Umph," I grunted, tripping over my own feet and falling face-first through the portal.

The walk through the portal was nothing like when Shade transported us places. There was no nausea, dizziness, or the incessant need to vomit everywhere. It was, however, incredibly disorienting to be the one who skidded across the grass at warp speed like someone had shot me out of a canon on the other side. I had never been more thankful that we didn't come out on a cement parking lot or a briar patch.

Groaning, I turned over and stared up at the sky. At first, I just glanced up nonchalantly, but then, the crystal clean air and vibrant teal above me caught me completely off guard. I'd never seen the sky so beautiful before. Shade walked up and leaned over, grinning at me. "You okay?"

I nodded and took his hand, letting him hoist me to my feet. I couldn't even get the words out of my mouth. All I could do was stare in all directions, taking in the wonder around me. We were in a lush green field with large stemmed purple flowers reaching up over our heads. Small creatures with tiny wings fluttered past us, and everything smelled sweet, like a candy store back home. The colors were so vibrant and beautiful I could barely look around with my dull human eyes. My brain was struggling to connect what I saw and the magnitude of it all.

Willa walked over and put her arm around my shoulders. "It's pretty, isn't it? I almost forgot how pretty it was here."

Shade looked around him curiously. "I've only been here a couple times, and I don't have a clue where we are."

Esmeralda took the pin out of her wild hair and shook it out. As she did, her appearance changed.

Magic fluttered all around her, her clothing changing, the wrinkles disappearing, and the look of old age faded away. Her skin was a beautiful porcelain white, and her hair, long and silky. "Why would you choose to look older back home?"

Esmeralda shrugged. "I just wanted people to leave me alone. Earth was interesting for like five seconds, but I needed to blend in."

I looked around her at Harry, who appeared pretty much the same, only his hair was longer, and he had somehow changed his clothes with magic. He was wearing clothes similar to what the fae guards had worn.

I turned to Willa. "You're not gonna magically change into someone else, too, are you? I'm gonna start getting really confused."

Willa giggled and shook her head. "Nah, I stayed the same. You and Shade, on the other hand...."

Shade let out an exhaustive sigh. He put out both arms and nodded. "Go ahead. I don't need any kind of attention drawn to me while I'm trying to figure this out."

Willa looked at her hands and scrunched her nose. "I think maybe we should wait until we get to the castle. I haven't used magic in a very long time, and I don't want to accidentally turn you into a tree or something.

Shade pursed his lips. "Probably a good call. Will we be okay until we get there?"

Willa narrowed her eyes and pushed two of the flowers blocking her view out of the way. She nodded ahead of her. "Yep. It looks like my sent the guard to pick us up. They'll make sure that we get in safely, and then the staff can change you."

Esmeralda and Harry hurried ahead, with Willa behind them, me trailing, and Shade bringing up the rear. I adjusted myself, pulling down on my shirt and brushing the twigs and dirt from my pants as we went. I wasn't really sure what to expect. In my head, I fully expected to walk through the field and have horses waiting for us to ride. Or maybe a pumpkin carriage… But that was just my silly fantasy books and stories from when I was a kid. Instead, sitting on the roadway at the edge of the field were two large black SUVs with guards standing next to them like secret service.

As soon as they saw us, they ushered us into the vehicles and shut the doors. I looked around, trying to find anything magic, but to be honest, it looked like a normal SUV.

Willa poked me in the side. "Why do you look disappointed?"

I shrugged. "It's really amazingly beautiful here, but I definitely wasn't expecting to be picked up in cars. It honestly kind of looks like Earth in Technicolor."

Willa chuckled. "It kind of is. I mean, the Pegasi were terribly expensive to take care of and hard to find. Once they got loose, there was no tracking device in them to find them. They raced off, never to be seen again."

I bit the inside of my cheek, wanting to ask about Pegasi but knowing that I needed to pace myself. I had a feeling there would be all kinds of things in the fae world that would throw me off-kilter. Instead, I looked out the window, watching as we drove along a beautiful scenic road and up a hill. As we crested, Esmeralda gasped and grinned. I followed her eyes up toward the horizon where an enormous castle, much like the one at Disney, sat glistening against the beautiful fae sky. I forcefully kept my mouth from gaping, knowing that I couldn't walk around like that for the rest of my time there. But it was just so beautiful.

I glanced over at Willa. "You're like freaking Cinderella."

She gave me an awkward smile, but her eyes stayed glued to the castle in the distance. "Yeah, except I broke my glass slippers a long time ago, and my fairy godmother... She turned out to be pretty lame."

It was at that moment, I realized that being back wasn't exactly thrilling to Willa. She had left for a reason, and with as quickly as she came when her aunt called, I could only imagine that it was a reason more than compelling. I reached out and put my hand over hers, giving her a kind smile when she glanced over at me. She squeezed my hand back, and we rode like that, looking out the window as I imagined what it would be like on the inside... and she remembered.

We sat back when we pulled into the large sparkling gates, letting the guards talk before pulling through. For some reason, I had it in my mind that there would be some huge welcoming party. An excited group of fae waiting to welcome back their princess. But that wasn't how it went. Instead, the SUVs pulled across the front and around the side of the castle, parking in a garage-like room. They quickly closed the doors behind them.

When we stopped, I looked over at Willa, confused. "There isn't some welcome-back party for you? You know, where people practice curtsying to the ground and children run up with flowers?"

Willa shook her head. "Not this time. We have to get you in before any of the staff sees you. Remember, your humanness has to stay quiet. Besides, my aunt will want to introduce me in another way. It has to be genteel and celebratory."

As the guard opened my door, I shook my head. "There are politics even in the fae world."

Willa rolled her eyes. "Unfortunately, there are politics in every world. It's part of the reason why I left."

I looked all around me in amazement as we walked through a long corridor and into the castle. Almost instantly, the scene changed from a plain white cement garage into a lavish and beautiful palace that I could've only imagined in a fairy tale. The floors were white marble and sparkled with every step that we took. Tapestries hung from the ceiling, and large pictures, taller than three of me standing one on top of the other, were anchored to the walls. Esmeralda and Harry seemed to know exactly where they were going, but Willa stayed by my side, with Shade just a few feet behind me. I couldn't see his face, but I could only imagine the suspicious caution he had.

We twisted and turned down multiple hallways and finally came to a stop at the first room, where Esmeralda happily hurried inside. Harry was put in the room across from her. We traveled down a little bit farther, and the guard stopped, motioning to Shade. He looked to Willa and back to me, obviously not wanting to leave my side just yet, but Willa gave him a comforting nod, and in he went. Behind him, two guards and what looked to be an older fae gentleman followed after them.

"What are they going to do to him?"

Willa giggled. "Nothing he's going to be happy about, but by the time they're done, he'll look like a member of the fae royal court."

At the end of the hallway, with five or six rooms between Shade and us, the guard stopped. Across the hall from each other were two sets of large wooden doors with beautiful carvings in them. One guard opened the door to my left and nodded to me, while another opened Willa's and bowed as she walked through. I stood, looking at her from across the hall, and before the door shut, she gave me a warm, comforting smile. Unfortunately, that smile was quickly interrupted when an older woman, maybe fae, but wild and frazzled like Esmeralda was before she got to the fae realm.

"Tsk, tsk, tsk. They did say this would be a challenge. Come on, dear, we've got to be done before dinner."

I raised a brow. "Is it going to hurt?"

The woman glanced at me for a second and then smiled. "Normally, I'd say no, but you're definitely all human."

And with that, she shut the door.

12

Callie

FROM THE TIME we arrived in the fae world to the moment I was escorted out of my room and down the hall, it was nothing but a whirlwind of magic, judgmental fae shaming, and a lot of curiosity as to what exactly I was going to look like what it was all done.

I pulled on the clothes she had given me, the woman they called the Magic Maker, and ran my hands over the soft material. I had never felt anything so delicate in my life. The fabric was incredibly light, the pants were fitted but comfortable, a blouse similar to silk, and a suit jacket that sparkled when I walked. They slipped my feet into a pair of soft flats and then stepped out of the way so I could see myself in the mirror.

Almost immediately, my mouth dropped open. It was me. I could see that my forty-year-old wrinkles had been smoothed out, my hair straightened and glistening, and my skin was porcelain white like Willa and her aunt. I recognized my body and my face, but everything was so much more delicate. Even though she didn't change how I moved, my body had a grace that I never had in the earthly realm. I lifted my perfectly sculpted brow and turned from side to side, noticing that she had also taken a bit off the sides. Then again, every fae I had seen so far was petite, slim, and almost perfect in appearance.

"That's even better than liposuction," I mumbled to myself. "If you ever get tired of the fae realm, I bet you could make a killing on Earth."

The Magic Maker shifted her eyeglasses onto the top of her head and wrinkled her nose. "I've been there. It's not my cup of tea. I like it here with the fae better."

"Aren't you a fae?"

She chuckled and pushed a piece of her curly

hair behind her ear. "I'm half-fae. The other half of me is a mystic."

Before I could ask her what exactly that meant, she started tugging on my clothes and stood back, nodding at me. "Try not to fiddle with your hands. Fae don't fiddle. And don't talk about humans. Or witches. If you don't know the answer to the question, just don't say anything at all. There will be plenty of people around you to make sure you don't get stuck. Luckily, fae lean more on their intuition than they do on their suspicions, and you have a strong fae feeling from the bracelet."

Nerves rattled in my stomach, and I suddenly realized that I would have to play a part. I was going to have to play a role that I knew nothing about. I wanted to protest, to tell her that it was pretty obvious I didn't know what I was doing and ask for help. But before I could, there was a knock on the door, and I found myself ushered out, following behind a guard toward another part of the castle.

"Where are we going?"

"Dinner with the princess," the guard said with a short, curt tone.

He definitely wasn't as friendly as the other fae, but I was just glad he wasn't the guy I had ac-

cidentally beaten up. Well, maybe it wasn't acci-
dental, but nonetheless, I definitely didn't want to
run into him. As we reached what I could only
assume was the dining room, the guard led me in.
Thankfully, there weren't a bunch of other fae
there. It was just Willa, her aunt, a man I didn't
recognize, my uncle, Shade, Esmeralda, and
Harry. They were all sitting around a large, long
oak table with food spread across the center and
candles lit all over the place.

Willa looked up and smiled, wearing something
similar to mine but in a purple color. Her hair was
no longer thoroughly dyed, and instead so blond it
was almost white, but just three-quarters of the
way down. The tips were a shimmering purple.
The whole fae world felt like a glitter bomb had
gone off, only it didn't stick to you and lay claim to
your cheek for the next five years. She patted the
seat next to her, and I hurried over, sitting down.
She leaned toward me and whispered. "Look at
you. A little magic, a little less spandex, and you
look like you finally had a good night's sleep."

I rolled my eyes. "Try a lot of magic."

Willa grinned and shifted her eyes across the
table. I followed her gaze and quickly pressed my
lips together, finding Shade sitting there, looking

slightly annoyed, his skin a fair white, his eyes blue, and his hair cropped short. It was blond like all the other fae, and his cheeks were suspiciously rosy. I wasn't about to call them out on it, though. He definitely fit right in, and while he was still incredibly handsome, I was more for the emo-witch look.

To his right was Willa's aunt, who gave me an approving nod and continued eating. Willa sat back and tugged on my shoulder. "This is my uncle. Uncle Bailey is my father's brother, the youngest of the three."

I could see Willa in her uncle. They had the same grin, the same chuckle, the same glisten in their eyes. It was something I couldn't see in Willa's aunt.

He reached his hand forward and shook mine. "So, you've been the best friend all these years. I've missed my little Willa so very much."

"That's me, though sometimes I think I'm less of a best friend and more of a hazard for her."

Willa shook her head. "Never. She's taken excellent care of me, Uncle. But I am so thrilled to see you."

I could tell there was a special bond between the two of them, and I could tell from the roll of her aunt's eyes that she wasn't as fond of Uncle Bailey as Willa was.

Her aunt cleared her throat and set down her fork, waving to the servants waiting for her to finish. "I'm sorry to eat and run, Willa, dear, but I have many things to attend to. We'll be holding a royal ball in celebration of your return. We believe that the event and the news will help strengthen the faith of the fae in their leaders. Until then, enjoy your time, and let me know if you need anything. There will be several fae coming to your room tomorrow to begin preparations for the ball in several days."

Willa nodded, and I smiled, but her aunt quickly pushed back the chair without noticing and hurried from the room. The room almost lightened tenfold as her aunt left. I leaned back in my chair, looking at the food they had set in front of me, and whispered to Willa. "Please tell me that there isn't a requirement for giant puffy sleeves and shimmering hoop skirts at the ball. And please tell me I don't have to put on a corset."

Willa cringed. "No corset, but it's definitely a tradition to wear a big puffy dress."

I groaned, leaning my head back. "I thought I had outlived the trauma of the 80s puffy sleeves."

Willa patted my leg. "It'll all be picked out for

you, don't worry. Now, eat. Your body isn't used to our realm. You're going to need to keep up with food. Besides, the fae have some of the best food in all the realms."

I lifted a brow. "I don't know... Have you ever tried old Ethel's pancake breakfast on Main Street?"

Willa laughed, and we all began to eat, talking amongst ourselves. It was nice, I had to admit. Even though I didn't fully look like myself, and I was trying to ignore the powerful waves of pulsating energy coming from my bracelet and palpitating through my entire body, I felt comfortable with friends. Maybe it was the fae, the calming magic that they all seemed to put out, but even Shade smiled and loosened up a little.

We stayed there for quite a while. I was a little bit confused about the time difference, but it didn't stop the yawning. By the time we got to our rooms, I was exhausted. When I went inside and locked the door behind me, I realized it was the first time I had time to take a good look at the place. It was beautiful. Everything was very modern-looking with clean lines and earth tones. The bed was enormous, and the mattress looked like a lumpy cloud sitting on a four-poster frame. I took off my fae suit and put on the pajamas sitting on the bed, shaking my head at how soft the material was. If they had material like that back on Earth, I would definitely broaden my wardrobe.

Climbing into bed, I rolled my eyes and groaned in ecstasy as I felt the softness envelop me. It was the most amazing mattress I had ever laid on. It literally felt like I had been wrapped in a cloud, while at the same time, everything was entirely supported. When I say it took me two seconds to fall asleep, I didn't even have time to think about it before I was long gone into a dream world.

I only wished that my dreams were as lovely as the comforter I had wrapped around me. But unfortunately, as I stirred in my dream state, I found myself standing in a large room, pillars jutting up in random patterns all around and the outer walls too far to see. I looked down at myself, finding I was dressed in a sparkling gown, only it looked like I had taken a run through the woods. The fabric was torn and dirty, and I reached up, feeling my hair pulled in all different directions.

In front of me, a figure moved, cloaked in a long black satin hooded robe. They didn't see me. Instead, they looked away as they shifted back and forth between the columns, making their way farther into the room. There was something inside of me, something that told me I needed to follow them. The energy pulsed on my wrist as I hurried along, trying to catch a glimpse of their faces. They slipped behind another column, but before I could follow, I was flanked. The enormously tall, robed creatures with red eyes that had attacked me in Rome came surging from all sides.

I reached between them as they pulled and shook me, trying to call out for the cloaked person, but nothing escaped my lips. I shoved, feeling my energy trying to erupt from the bracelet, but the red-eyed beings were too much. The cloaked person disappeared into the darkness just as I was overcome by the shrouded figures.

My eyes immediately shot open, my breath heavy in my chest. I fully expected to see nothing more than darkness in the room, but to my surprise, the windows were open, and the sun was shining inside. The dream felt like it had only taken a few seconds, but my body was well-rested, and it was definitely morning. Something rustled behind me. I turned over in bed, pulling the blanket up around my chest.

One of the fae servants was hanging up an outfit for me.

She curtsied to me, and her eyes went to the floor. "I'm sorry. Breakfast is ready, and the others are on their way there right now. Princess Willa sent over a hand-picked outfit for you that she thought you'd be more comfortable in today. I will wait outside and if you need anything, let me know."

I nodded and smiled at her, watching her leave the room. Why didn't they wake me up earlier? There was no way that I could get ready that fast. If they were already on their way to breakfast, by the time I brushed my hair, put on makeup, and got dressed, they'd be done. I figured I had no choice but to make do, so I pulled the covers back and got out of bed, stretching my shoulders and my back. I hadn't felt that good in an exceedingly long time. I definitely didn't feel forty, and in fact, didn't even feel twenty. I could definitely get used to that.

I hurried over and took the clothes, smiling at the outfit that Willa had sent. It was a pair of black riding pants, which I assumed was the closest thing she could find to yoga pants, a white flowing blouse, and a pair of knee-high brown boots. I tossed my pajamas onto the chair and quickly got dressed, preparing myself for the mess I usually was in the morning when I looked in the mirror. I would say that my normal morning appearance was somewhere between zombie and Medusa.

However, as I dipped in front of the mirror, I chirped in the excitement. I had forgotten completely about my fae appearance. Apparently, fae could sleep all night and not have a single tangle in their hair or smudge of makeup. It looked like I had spent hours getting ready.

I could definitely get used to that.

By the time I made it to breakfast, Willa's aunt had already left, and Willa was finishing up. Shade and my uncle were sitting at the table, on the other end, chatting to each other. Willa took a quick sip of her coffee and patted her lips as she stood up, reaching her hand for me. "I'm sorry I couldn't wait. I have so many things that I have to do today. But the three of you will be shown to the library. I figured you could start there with your research, and I'll join you as soon as I can. I don't really have control over these things right now, but after the ball, things will settle down."

My heart did a little patter of excitement. "Please tell me the library here is just as amazing as the rest of the castle. I'm talking puts *Beauty and the Beast* to shame. I'll never want to leave. You're gonna have to build a restaurant inside and put a cot in there because it's that good."

She leaned in and whispered with a big smile. "It's even better. In fact, I spent many, many years there in the fantasy creature section as a child. It was always my favorite. There was this one book that I literally read so many times that my father had to magically rebind it so that it could stay on the shelf. I think it was called *The Lore of the Mystics*. They were stories about these amazingly powerful beings that were very prevalent long before I came. By the time I was born, though, there was mostly just mixed blood and a few of the older mystics left, but they've died out since. The woman who helped you was part mystic. It was a great book."

I leaned in and kissed her cheek. "Go do princess stuff, and thanks for the clothes. And by the way, I saw how easily I got up, and my hair was done... I'm on to you."

One of the guards cleared his throat, and Willa chuckled, sticking out her bottom lip to me and waving as she hurried off after him. Alabaster and Shade were already standing up, readying themselves for the library. I didn't want anybody to wait on me, so I grabbed a croissant off the table and took a sip of water.

"We can wait for you," Shade said.

"Nope, I'm good. I don't usually eat breakfast anyway. Besides, I'm being escorted to a fae library. That's worth missing like a week's worth of meals."

Alabaster chuckled, and Shade rolled his eyes. "What is it with girls and libraries?"

As we followed along behind one of the servants, I tapped him on the shoulder and leaned in. "It's because we're smarter than you. We understand that there are big words that boys have a hard time reading."

Alabaster let out a very jolly laugh that echoed down the hall. Shade turned and looked at me as we followed along, narrowing his eyes. I was struggling to tell whether he was flirting with me or just joking around. Shade was still just as hard to read as a fae as he was as a witch. That was definitely not something they had changed.

We rounded the corner and came to a stop as the servant pulled open the two doors and stepped to the side, putting his arm out. We slowly walked around the corner and into the library, my face stunned and my arms falling limp at my sides. I had never seen anything like it before. The walls were covered in shelving, and there were at least four floors with a dome ceiling at the top. There were tables sparsely set around the room, and at the back were even more rows of books. I couldn't even tell how far back it went.

Rubbing my hands together, I nudged Shade to the side. "Now, this is more my speed."

13

Callie

WE SPENT hours at the library that first day.

I probably walked ten miles and had only just begun to understand the sheer number of books on the first floor, let alone the entire place. I had my speed walk on, weaving and bobbing through the stacks, pulling down books, and forcing myself not to ooh and ahh at every title I came to. The mall walkers of America would have been proud of me.

Alabaster, Shade, and I tackled the bottom floor, all different sections, all looking for the same things. We were researching the stone to understand more about it, what it did, and the powers it held. We were also looking for the King Collector or any kind of creature that resembled him. Of course, we really didn't know much about what he looked like except for my small memory of him, but we knew what his cronies looked like.

There were stacks and stacks of books about the different magical creatures, dark magic, and everything in between splayed out on the tables. However, after hours of research, we still had no idea who the King Collector was or where he might've come from. We were coming up completely empty, which didn't make any sense to me. Either a whole new level of being was created without anyone knowing it in any of the realms, or there was something much more common about the King Collector than we realized. Either way, Shade was getting antsy, and I could tell he wasn't the kind of guy who was satisfied with doing research in the library.

Walking out of one of the stacks, reading a book, I glanced up to find him pacing the floor, seemingly talking to himself. I stopped and raised a brow. "I know that we're free to use the library, but I'm pretty sure that Willa will be pissed if you run a hole in the carpet. You might want to relax."

Shade stopped and glanced up at me, realizing he was talking to himself. He chuckled and let out an exhaustive sigh. "I can't look at another book. I now know every creature ever born in any realm outside of Earth. Not a single one of them has anything to do with the King Collector. And if they do? We don't know what it is. I feel like I'm just wasting time here." He grabbed his light-weight jacket from the back of the chair. "I'm gonna do some research on my own out in town. I'll let you know if I come up with anything. If you find anything in those books..."

I nodded. "I'll let you know. Be safe out there."

He gave me a half-smile and then turned and walked from the library. I looked back at Alabaster with my hands on my hips. "Well, I guess it's just the two of us."

But Alabaster wasn't paying any attention to me. He was standing there, mumbling to himself like a crazed professor. I couldn't even understand what he was saying. He glanced at me and put up his finger, hurrying from the room after Shade. I blinked, finding myself standing alone in the library, surrounded by open books, abandoned for a more exciting version of research.

With a sigh, I grabbed a stack of the books and started toward the shelving, figuring I could at least put things back the way they were when we had found them.

I started out with a stack of Shade's books and paused as I passed the children's section, remembering what Willa had said about her favorite book. I knew it was wasting time, but I didn't know a lot about Willa, especially her childhood, and I felt like she wouldn't have told me that if she didn't want me to look for it. I set the stack of books on a small table and walked into the more whimsical area that looked to be decorated just for Willa. There were cutouts, floating in midair, almost dancing around above my head. They were all ballerinas and princesses, and if I listened close enough, I could hear faint giggles coming from them.

Each bookshelf in the circular area was smaller than the central area, only coming up to my waist. Each one was labeled with a letter, making it easier for Willa to find the books she wanted. First, I went over to *L*, looking for lore. Still, when I didn't find it, I skipped right over to *M*, scanning the shelves until about halfway down when I saw the repaired spine of a book that I couldn't read the title because it was so worn out.

I carefully pulled it from the shelf and wiped my hand across the cover, finding a beautiful illustration of a woman wielding magic on the front, entitled *The Lore of the Mystics*.

Glancing around me, I saw a small space in the corner with a mat that looked to be worn down. I could already imagine a tiny version of Willa sitting in the corner with this book open for the 10,000th time, reading through the pages, letting her imagination run wild as she dreamed of other realms and what her future might hold.

I meandered over and squatted in the same spot, grunting as I sat, remembering that I wasn't quite young and spry anymore, despite the magic that cloaked my wrinkles. No matter how much magic they used, I could still hear my bones creak, and my joints screamed at me. Once I was finally settled and breathing again, I began to flip through the book. When I reached about midway, I stopped and smiled, instantly recognizing an illustration meant to be a beautiful fae princess. She even looked kind of like Willa. I held the book up in front of me, trying to get a better look since the lighting in the room was terrible. As I lifted it, a piece of paper fluttered out of the back and onto the floor.

Glancing down, I could see the parchment

folded and Willa's name carefully written on the front. My first thought was that the note was something Willa had written as a child and shoved into the back of her favorite book. It was probably a seriously terrible breach of privacy, but I wanted to know what Willa was like in her former life before the bookstores and hair dye. I set the book down and carefully opened the letter.

As soon as I saw the first line, I knew that Willa hadn't written it.

Dear Willa,

If you're reading this, things are far worse than I imagined. My dearest daughter, if you are reading this, then I am not there with you, and you're in an incredible amount of danger...

14

Shade

As I walked through the maze of hallways in the fae castle, toward pretty much any door that I could find outside, I passed by a mirror. As soon as I stepped beyond it, I paused, backing up and wrinkling my nose at my reflection.

It was probably an excellent thing that I didn't bring any witches with me because I would never live down the fact that they had turned me into one of them. Well, one of them without their intense powers. My own power still worked in the fae world, but it wasn't quite as awe-inspiring as it was on Earth.

My lip curled, and I shivered, tearing my eyes away from my own unrecognizable reflection. At the end of the hall, two balcony doors sat open with a wide staircase leading down into the gardens.

Before I could reach the door, I heard a shuffling behind me and paused, looking over my shoulder. Alabaster was hurrying down, seemingly talking to himself but definitely following me. I really didn't want company. I wanted to do my thing, but I also knew that a finder could be beneficial in a place that I was very unfamiliar with. I knew how to get to the town, but I really didn't know anything other than that.

It had been a very long time since I had been to the fae world, and even when I was there, we weren't really allowed to go places because we were there on royal duty.

"Alabaster, why don't you stay with Callie? She's your family, after all."

His lips were moving, and his eyes shifted up toward mine. "You seek the stone, but to find the stone, you have to find the thief."

I shrugged. "That's one way of doing it. Why? You know where I can find this thief?"

He shook his finger in the air and began to walk out the door, still talking. I groaned and followed after him, having to pick up the pace to keep up with them. "Clues. I have clues. Secret rhymes and bubbling brews stack the shelves of the place you may find clues."

I lifted both brows. "Finders talk in rhyme as well?"

Alabaster narrowed his eyes at me, and I shook my head, putting up my hands.

"Right, so... secret rhymes and brews... a bar?"

"No, no," Alabaster said, shaking his head dramatically.

I snapped my fingers and pointed at him. "An apothecary."

I rubbed my chin, thinking about my time walking through the town, the one time I had been there as a kid. Almost everything in the fae town was pretty simple. It was much like Earth, but almost everything was handmade. The fae didn't have corporations and lawyers. They had magic and community.

I turned back to Alabaster. "There's an apothecary in the middle of the town. I remember seeing it as a kid. I'm not sure it'll still be there. I had only glimpsed it in passing because it was down an alleyway. It was between a shop that sold clothing and one that sold scrolls."

"Bingo," he replied to me with a big grin.

With that, we took off, heading back around the castle and out the front gate. I kept my head down, not even looking at the guards as I passed. For some reason, it felt weird, like I was escaping, but I wasn't their prisoner. They just wanted us to be careful. The town was at the base of the hill, edging up to the cliffs that overlooked a large body of clear, calm water. Overhead, several large dragons flew by, shadowing our path for just a moment before their bodies uncovered the sun.

The town was busier than I had remembered, but that was so long ago there were probably a lot more fae. But the realm of the fae wasn't just for them. It was a place that all magical creatures came, especially the capital city. A lot of business was done there, travelers came there for sightseeing, and people with business with the royal family came there. Then there were the locals, the shop owners, and farmers. If it weren't for the fact that the fae hated the witches and vice versa, the fae realm, in my opinion, was better than Earth. Yeah, there's a lot of darkness in the fae realm and many things that go on in the shadows that people don't know, but not nearly as bad as Earth. At least the fae valued the lives of the other fae.

Everything looked exactly as I had remembered it. The streets were the same paving stones. The buildings were all the same color, with moss growing on the roofs—the same two stores sat on opposite sides of an alleyway right where I remembered the shop being. When we stopped, we both glanced around as if we were doing something wrong and slipped into the shadows of the alley. I shoved my hands into my pockets, and Alabaster did the same, heading down the dew-filled, rather musky alley to find a small brown dirty door with a hand-etched sign hanging from it that read *Apothecary*.

Seeing it in the alley close up, it was shocking that I had even noticed it as a kid riding past. Then again, I noticed everything when I was a kid. There was something about the place that gave me the creeps. It definitely looked like a place I would find a thief. I slowly and quietly opened the door, peeking inside. There were rows and rows of shelves lining the walls, tables containing little trinkets and bottles, skulls of animals long since passed on one side, and candles on the other. There was an herbal smell emanating from a small smoking dish that floated in the center of the room.

We didn't see anybody behind the counter, at least. So, we quietly moved around the room, looking at the different things. The place reminded me of a mixture of a new age shop in an antique store back on Earth, and I wondered what somebody would do with so many tiny, fragile glass vials. Alabaster tapped me furiously on the shoulder at the back of the store, pulling me over to a table. He leaned toward me and whispered, "These are old school. Many of the things they're selling in here are actually illegal in the fae world."

I picked up one of the bottles and sneered at the picture of the silhouette witch flying on a broomstick across the moon. "I can see they still have no idea what witches actually are."

Alabaster shook his head. "Look at this one. This potion will freeze an enemy for fifteen seconds, and you only need to use one drop of it. It's been illegal for centuries. How easy would it be to just drop this on your enemies all at one time and take them out before they could move? I remember it was used on members of the royal house long ago, and that's when they outlawed it."

The sound of whispering hit my ears, and I glanced over at a thick, velvety curtain covering the doorway. I inched closer, keeping my back pressed against the bookcase, leaning around just enough to see through the crack. There were two people back there. One was fully covered in a cloak with the hood pulled up and faced away from me. The other an older gentleman with wrinkles at the corners of his eyes and a frown that I was pretty sure was permanent. He was definitely not a fae, but he might have been a mystic or at least a half one.

The older gentlemen wore brown trousers, tattered brown boots with the toe rubbed, a striped button-up shirt folded to his elbows, and a brown vest with the chain of a pocket watch hanging from the front. He had a large handlebar mustache that covered his upper lip's entirety, and his hair was thinning and parted deeply on the side, attempting to cover up his bald spot. He looked nervous, his hands clenched at his sides.

Alabaster turned toward me, but I put my hand up, pressing one finger to my lips and shaking my head.

"We already have the stone," the cloaked figure whispered. "It is safely hidden right under their noses. But not for long."

The old man snarled, "It's about time things changed."

I leaned forward just a bit more, but in my haste, my elbow hit a small iron pan, no bigger than the palm of my hand, and I flipped it off the shelf. I tried to juggle to catch it, but there was no way I could, and it clattered loudly on the floor. Immediately I pulled back, and my eyes went wide. The cloaked figure raced out of the back and out of sight. I wanted to chase the person, but we needed to get out of the apothecary even more so. I didn't know who the shop owner was or what kind of part he played in all of it. The last thing we needed was for him to make out who we were.

Grabbing Alabaster by the arm, we hurried out of the shop, shutting the door carefully behind us, and then raced down the alleyway around the corner. We pressed our backs against the brick front of the store, facing the road, and listened as the shop owner came hurrying out and looked up and down the alley. I carefully peeked around the corner, watching him, wondering how far he would go to see who had been inside the shop. However, after a few minutes, he grumbled and grunted, waving his hand angrily in the air and headed back into a shop.

"We should get back," Alabaster said. "We've seen all we will see here."

I nodded at him, a hollow feeling simmering in my stomach. I looked around the corner again to make sure the old man hadn't come back out, and we hurried back toward the castle. The entire time my mind was running wild, trying to figure out what in the world that all meant. Whoever the cloaked figure was, they said something about the stone being right under our noses, which meant that they had to be in the castle as well. But there were so many people in the fae castle it would be impossible to figure out who it was.

When we got back, we hurried inside and down toward our rooms. Callie turned the corner, walking straight toward us, looking down at something in her hands.

"Hey."

She glanced up at me and held out the paper. "I found something. It's strange. It's a letter that was in the back of Willa's favorite childhood book. It basically says that if Willa's reading that things are far worse than the person imagined. I think her father wrote it, and I don't think it was that long ago. He talks about danger within the castle but then the letter trails off and was left unfinished. Maybe somebody was coming and he had to stop and put the letter in the book. What I do know is that Willa's safety is at risk."

I held the parchment in my hand, reading the few sentences that had been written, and it definitely sparked something, making what I had heard in the apothecary all too coincidental. At the same time, though, I couldn't be sure. It was dark and quiet in there, and it was hard to hear what they were saying in the back room. The last thing I wanted to do was send the fae looking in the wrong direction and have something happen to their princess. It wouldn't bode very well for me, either, considering I was a witch in fae clothing.

Callie took the letter back and looked at it, biting her bottom lip. Her sparkling eyes stared up at me.

I had this unyielding urge to pull her into my arms and hug her, but I tightened my hands into fists in my pockets and kept myself at a distance. "What are you going to do?"

She thought about it for a second and glanced over Alabaster. "I think I should go to Willa's aunt and let her know what I found. I know she'll be able to keep Willa safe."

At that point, I wasn't sure we could trust anyone, but I couldn't tell Callie that; it would only worsen her fear. I'd have to keep an eye on both of them, and when the secret was revealed, we'd see where the chips fell.

15

Callie

STANDING NERVOUSLY in the center of the dimly lit room where Willa's aunt spent most of her time, I watched as she paced back and forth, studying the letter.

I was usually pretty good at reading people, but the queen regent was an expert at hiding her emotions. I guess it came with the territory when you lived and breathed the royal life. There were only a few lines written on the page. Still, I stood there for what felt like forever as she read and reread the text, pacing back and forth as the fire in the fireplace sent off dancing shadows across the room.

It was an eerie feeling that I hadn't had since I was in Rome. I pushed it back, knowing it was probably just because I was worried about Willa and I knew there was danger right there in the castle. After several more moments and me tilting from side to side, glancing around the room for the 800th time, her aunt turned around and folded her arms over her chest.

She stared into the flames of the fire as she talked. "It's unreal. I loved my brother, but I don't understand why he wouldn't have come to me beforehand if he were afraid of something. Why would he have left a half-written note in the back of a book that he didn't know if his daughter would ever get?"

I wasn't sure if that was a rhetorical question or not, but I decided to answer anyway. "It could've been several things. Maybe it doesn't mean anything. Maybe it means that he wrote that, not knowing that one day this would happen, but because he's royalty, he knew there was a chance. He could've gotten interrupted and slipped it into the book and then just forgotten about it…. There are so many things it *could* mean."

Willa's aunt looked at me, knowing full well that I didn't believe a word I was saying.

I offered another suggestion. "Maybe he didn't know who to trust, and when fear takes you over, it can cloud your judgment. Maybe it messed with his head. The lines got blurred, like paranoia. Or maybe he didn't come to you because he didn't want to put you in danger. You are his little sister, after all. I don't have any siblings, but I always assumed if I did, I would do everything to protect them."

Her eyes shifted away from the fire and down to the floor. I immediately regretted saying that. I didn't regret it because it could have possibly been the truth, but because I could see the sadness seep over her. She kept that look for several seconds and then straightened herself up, hardening her expression again. The smile she had given us at the house had long since stopped, and I was seeing who Willa's aunt truly was. The funny thing was, with the tingle up my arm from the bracelet and her expressionless face, I really had no more clues as to what she thought than I did for the first time I open the door to her.

"You did the right thing, Callie. Thank you for coming to me with this. I'm going to get some of my best guards on the situation and ensure the castle is the safest it can be." She took several steps toward me, and I clutched my hands tighter in front. "I do have to ask that you not say anything to Willa about this right now. I think waiting until after the ball, once things have quieted down and we can freely look into it, would be better than telling her now. She's distracted and stressed. This would only add to it. I want her mind to be as clear as possible so that if something does happen, she's able to think."

It felt weird to hide something from my best friend, but at the same time, that's what I'm supposed to do if it kept her safe. At least that's what I thought. She had done that for me by not telling me about fae for all those years. All I had to do was keep a secret from her until after the ball. It wasn't like I could spend any time with her anyway, so I didn't see it as a problem.

Finally, I nodded and gave in to her smile. "Not until after the ball. I promise."

That fake smile settled back onto her lips, further chilling my uncomfortableness in that room. I could tell she wanted me to be gone, and I wasn't going to argue with her. I didn't want to be in that space one second longer, and I didn't know why. I headed back to my room and readied myself for dinner, nervous that I would have to stare Willa in the face and not tell her something about her own safety. I didn't know how she had done it for all those years.

However, when I got to the dining room, a smaller one than the banquet hall we had been in before, I realized I wouldn't even have to worry about that because Willa couldn't come to dinner. Apparently, she had a lot of things to take care of before the ball. She was actually coming out of the dining room when I was going in.

I put a big smile on my face. "Hey there! You look stressed. Are you okay?"

Willa didn't break into her normal grin, which was an immediate alarm for me, but I didn't want to read too much into it. I had never seen Willa under so much pressure before, so it was only normal that she would have an adverse reaction. She shrugged and glanced over at the guard, giving them a nod. "It is what it is."

And then she left me standing there by myself. That was probably the most challenging and weirdest part of the whole conversation. It was one line back and forth to each other, and then she walked off as if she were talking randomly to a stranger in a grocery store. I didn't like the feeling it gave me, but what could I do about it? Willa was being prepped to take her spot as queen regent, and it was something that Willa didn't want. On top of that, her father was missing, and so was a very important stone for the entire fae realm—possibly for all the realms.

I gathered myself and headed into the dining room, finding Alabaster and Shade sitting at a table with plates in front of them. They hadn't touched their food, and Shade stood as I walked in. It was strange, and I could tell he thought it was strange, too, because his cheeks went red, and he cleared his throat, slowly sitting back down. It was like he had a burst of chivalry, but his body quickly rejected it.

Not wanting to make a big deal about it, I sat down and smiled at one of the servants as they brought me dinner. I picked up my fork and pushed the beans around, my mind somewhere else.

"Your uncle gave me a clue today or hinted at where I could find clues."

I had completely forgotten to ask Shade and Alabaster what they had found in the city. "Really? Did you figure it out?"

Shade nodded as he swallowed. "We ended up at apothecary down an alleyway in town. We went inside, and it was a bunch of empty vials and books and potions that were apparently illegal to sell in the fae realm. But there was also this curtain to the back room, and while we were at the back, we overheard two people whispering to each other. There was an older gentleman and then a hooded figure, but I couldn't see their face."

A hooded figure...

Flashes of my dream came back to me, but I didn't say anything. It was a dream. After all, I didn't want to sound like the crazy one. I was starting to think I was going insane. Between the fae realm and the reflection in the mirror that I could barely identify as me, I could feel the pressure starting to rise in my chest. It was just so odd that my dream was so similar to that. We spent most of the rest of dinner silent, picking at the food on our plates while our minds wondered whatever questions we were trying to answer.

When my uncle finished, he pushed back from the table and blotted his lips with his napkin. "I'm going back to the library to do some more research."

I glanced around. "Where's Tiny?"

Alabaster put both hands on his knees and grunted as he stood up. "He's got family in the area, so I let him go spend some time with them. I don't really need him here. I'm not really under any danger in this realm, not like I was on Earth. I'll let you know if I find anything at the library."

I gave him the best smile I could muster, which probably looked pretty awkward and bordered on creepy. I was never particularly good at faking my emotions. "I think I'm going to take a little bit of a break. One of the servants mentioned that I should see the nighttime gardens. Apparently, they glow and dance when the moon comes out."

My uncle smiled. "They are beautiful. Just be careful. We don't know who this cloaked figure is or if they're anywhere near us."

"I'll go with her," Shade said, tossing his napkin onto his empty plate. "I could use the walk to clear my mind."

We ambled slowly down the steps and along the lit walkway toward the back gardens. I held my hands in front of me nervously, unsure of why Shade was coming with me. I knew he wanted to keep me safe, but I felt like there was more to it than that; at least there was to me. As I walked, my thoughts were consumed by him, that was until I rounded the corner and saw the opulence and glow of the night gardens. They were stunning and appeared as if someone had lit the entire garden with sparkling lights and glow-in-the-dark paint. However, as I grew closer, I realized that everything in the space sparkled and glowed independently. It was an entire ecosystem of intricately grown plants and flowers that moved and opened as we passed.

I gasped at the beauty every five seconds, shaking my head at the wonder in front of me. Small specks of light lifted from the leaves of the plants and shimmered all around us. I felt as if I were walking through space with millions of stars and glowing planets passing by as I walked. A light chuckle from Shade drew my attention.

I glanced over at him and wrinkled my nose in embarrassment. "What? Can a girl not be completely enamored by this place?"

He smiled and gave me a short nod. "Of course you can. I was enamored by this place when I first saw it as well. I thought it was just magic. I thought the fae had enchanted this garden, but it's just part of this realm. It's hard not to love everything about it."

There was a pain in his voice, and I knew that the fae realm was bittersweet to him between his missing brother and the attack when he was younger. I had only been there a short time, and it was bittersweet to me as well. It was almost as if I couldn't even trust the beauty around me because I wasn't sure where its loyalties laid. Nonetheless, at that moment, I just wanted to enjoy it.

We wandered down and through the paths and had no idea of the amount of time we had been in there, but it didn't matter to me. When we reached the middle of the garden, it opened up to a fountain in the center. Illuminated water spirals seemed to defy gravity as they twisted up and around the pillar and flowed from the top. Glowing lily pads gave off a neon ring in the water as they floated gently around the bowl of the fountain.

I sat on the edge and looked down, watching my reflection waver in the water below. I could see Shade's reflection as well, but not the Shade that I had come to know. He was the fae version of the witch that had originally kidnapped me. He sat down next to me, running his fingers along the water's edge.

I kept my eyes on our reflections as I spoke. "I want you to know that I'm not naïve. I can see through the beauty of this place. I'm starting to see the secrets you were talking about. They're such strange things going on here."

"What do you mean?" he asked.

"Hooded figures, enormous libraries, half-written notes from a missing king—it's a huge, messy puzzle, and we're not even sure if we have all the pieces or what the final picture will be."

"Wait... Did you just say a hooded figure?"

I looked up at him, finding the startled look on his face surprising. I forgot that I hadn't told him about my dream, but I guess I kinda had to at that point. He was going to think it was stupid. In fact, a day removed from the actual dream, and I thought it was stupid as well. After all, the last dream I remembered having before that was Shade—but with Bean's head—drooling on me. I couldn't really put a lot of stock into what happened when I was asleep.

I took a deep breath and turned toward him, clutching my hands in my lap. As I went to answer, I was cut off by the sound of loud blowing horns coming from the castle. Shade immediately stood up and looked around, the tension back in his shoulders, and his senses perked. I didn't understand what was happening.

"Has someone arrived at the castle?"

Shade shook his head as he scanned our surroundings. "No. Those are alarm calls." He reached down, his face serious. "We need to get you back inside."

I stood up with him and began to walk, feeling

his hand tighten around my wrist as he pulled me along.

I shook my head and grabbed him, stopping him in his tracks. "What's going on?"

He looked back at the castle and then at me. "Someone's been attacked, and it's inside the castle walls."

Callie

MY FIRST THOUGHT was immediately Willa.

As soon as the words came out of his mouth, I was racing down the path, leaving him behind. I could hear his footsteps behind me but didn't stop to look back as I took the steps two at a time up the balcony and in through the side door of the castle.

I stopped when I got inside and looked around, determining what was happening and where it was coming from. I raced through the kitchen and out the door into the hallway, fig-

uring I would make my way to Willa's room because it was most likely where she was. However,
as I turned to head toward our living quarters, a
large group of servants came rushing down the
hallway in the opposite direction.

One of the servants was the girl who had been
waking me up in the morning, and I quickly
reached out and grabbed her, pulling her back.
"What's going on? Is the princess…"

The girl was breathing heavily, and she shook
her head. "No, Princess Willa is safely guarded in
her room. This is in the library. It was the finder.
He was attacked."

I let go of her wrist, and she ran off, but I
couldn't move. My heart flip-flopped in my chest,
and all I could think about was that Alabaster was
the last remaining relative that I knew of, and I
hadn't even gotten to fully know him yet. Shade
hurried next to me, shaking his head as he caught
his breath. "Willa?"

My face stayed still, my eyes locked on the
path toward the library. "No. She's safe. They said
Alabaster was attacked."

I knew he was reaching out and touching my
arm, but all the nerves in my body had gone still,
and I barely knew how to breathe.

"Is he alive?"

I blinked several times, pulling myself out from the trance, and looked up at Shade. I realized I hadn't even asked that question. My mind automatically assumed he wasn't, but I had no idea. His eyes fluttered over my face, and I could see that he was reading that exact thought in my mind.

He pressed his lips together and put his hand against my back. "Let's go see. We'll go together."

Without him there, I probably wouldn't have been able to move from that spot. My feet felt like lead. The closer we got to the library, the closer the dread filled me. I hadn't realized until that moment how important it was to me that I had found another family member. For a second, I didn't feel like an orphan. We made our way to the library, pushing through the crowd of servants gathered, nervously looking through the doors. Several guards carried a stretcher with Alabaster lying unconscious on it as we reached the doors, his body bruised, blood trickling from the edge of his mouth.

Slowly I reached out, afraid to touch his hand, afraid to feel the coldness of death. But when my skin met his, I felt warmth, and I immediately knew he was still living. Tears pulled at the edge of my eyes, and I looked up at Shade, who gave me a half-smile and nodded. We followed them through the castle to the medical wing, where we were stopped short as they took him into an examination room. I stared at the doors, biting the inside of my lip, afraid to look away because I didn't want to miss something.

I wasn't sure if ten minutes had passed or ten hours because I was stuck in that warp, the tunnel straight to my uncle lying in the other room.

When the doctor finally came through, or whatever they called fae medical people, she smiled kindly, trails of magic finishing from her fingertips. "He's going to be okay, but I think it's going to take a while. Looks like he was attacked by some magical creature, but it wasn't just a magical attack. They physically attacked him as well. It appears they used some sort of freezing magic, something that left him vulnerable to the attack. There are no signs that he fought back."

I swallowed hard. "Is he awake?"

The doctor shook her head. "I administered some magic that will keep him calm and comfortable so his body can heal better. His wounds were pretty traumatic, and even my magic couldn't fully heal him. He did, however, have a book clutched in his hands. I wasn't sure if it was his or from the library, but I took it, and I figured you might want to have it back... at least until he wakes up."

I nodded, watching as she pulled a small green book from her front pocket and handed it to me. There were fingerprints of blood from where my uncle had gripped it tightly. Shade put his hand on my shoulder and smiled at the fae doctor. "Thank you. If anything changes, if you could let us know, that would be great. We'll come back in the morning and see how he's feeling."

She smiled and bowed slightly, turning and going back through the doors. I was in a bit of a trance, so Shade guided me down the hallways and back toward our bedrooms. He opened my door to let me in, going in first just to look around for safety. I stood there in the center of the room, clutching the book to my chest, trying to work through everything in my mind. I was frankly kind of shocked that Willa hadn't even come out of her room yet. Surely, she knew about what had happened.

Then again, someone had attacked Alabaster, and they didn't know where the person—or creature—had run off to. Ultimately that meant Willa's life could be at risk. We didn't need two of us going down, and who knew what we could expect from the coming days.

Shade walked over to me and put his hand on my shoulder, shaking me out of it yet again. "I don't want you to leave the room tonight, okay? I'm going to be right down the hall, and I'll come to check on you. I'll at least listen in to make sure that you're okay. Lock the door, don't answer without knowing who's on the other side, and if you need anything, just call for me."

I smiled, patting him on the chest. "Thanks, Dad. Should I carry my pepper spray?"

He furrowed his brow and put his hands on his hips. "It's not funny."

I groaned, rolling my eyes. "I know. I know! I have this terrible habit of inappropriate humor when I'm nervous."

In a move that I didn't see coming, he reached over and pulled me in, wrapping his arms around me in a hug. It was strange at first, but the magic surged up my arm and across my chest, and I laid my head against his shoulder, letting out a deep sigh. Slowly, he pulled back, but when our eyes met, he quickly averted and turned, heading for the door. He glanced back at me with an awkward smile as he shut it. I could tell he was waiting on the other side until I locked the two deadbolt locks.

If it hadn't been for everything going on at that moment, I would've been incredibly frustrated, but I had too much on my mind. The last thing I needed to think about was Shade's inability to decide whether he liked me or he didn't like me. I was forty years old, and I was playing games with him. I wasn't playing games on purpose. It was just like a cat chasing a mouse, but suddenly the mouse turns on the cat, and it was back and forth over and over again.

Slipping off my boots, I headed over to the bed and plopped down, lying back. I pulled the book out and opened it up, reading the first couple of pages. I realized quickly it was no different from the five million other magical beast books we had looked at in the library. I had to admit, I was kind of irritated by it. I thought for sure there'd be something, a clue, anything in the book. But it seemed he had just clutched on to the first thing he could find when he was attacked.

I flipped through to the last page and was about to close it when I saw a golden-color ink on the very last page. It wasn't printed like the other text and instead hand-drawn. It was a knot, like the Celtic knot, except this one was very familiar. I sat up and looked closer at it, tracing my finger over the lines. I knew I had seen that symbol somewhere before, somewhere in passing maybe. Maybe the book wasn't useless after all. Maybe he had clutched it because of the mark on the last pages. There had to be something to its familiarity, and it wasn't anything I had researched or experienced back on Earth.

I replayed the time I had been in the fae realm back in my mind, searching for that symbol that I knew was somewhere in there. Suddenly, startling me to the point where I almost fell off the bed, a loud knock echoed wildly through the room. I closed the book and put it under my pillow, straightening out the blankets over top of it. Hurrying over to the door, I grabbed the door handle but leaned against it. "Who's there?"

There was a sound of shuffling on the other side, but no one said a word. My heart began to race louder in my chest, and slowly I backed away a few steps, narrowing my eyes. Shade said not to trust anyone coming to the door unless I knew who it was. Whoever was standing out there, though, they either couldn't hear me or didn't want me to hear them. I looked all around the room, but I was trapped. Would the attacker really knock on the door? Unfortunately, the question had been coming up far too many times in recent weeks.

With my breathing increased and my heart racing, I closed my eyes and focused on the energy flowing through me. I had given in to the comfort of knowing that Shade was there to protect me. But I didn't need saving. Whoever was standing on the other side of that door either meant me harm or not, but I wasn't going to find out cowering in my room.

Hopefully, I wasn't making a terrible mistake. Mistakes in the fae world all seemed to end in either near-death or complete annihilation. I liked those tropes in movies, but not in my own life.

17

Callie

Iᴛ's times like these that I wish I had that flat iron again.

Mustering my bravery, or my stupidity, I grabbed the handle of the door. I yanked it open, practically wheezing with my hands balled into fists, ready to attack whoever was on the other side. But on the other side wasn't some secret cloaked nemesis.

Instead, there was a giant ball of fabric wiggling around until one of the servants poked her head up over the top of it. She started out with an immediate smile. As her eyes rolled over my intense, very ridiculous defense pose, her smile fell.

"I'm really sorry for bothering you so late, but I needed to bring your dress over for the ball. You don't need to do anything. I just need to hang it up in your room."

I glanced at my hands and dropped them to my sides, standing up straight. I could feel the flush of my cheeks from embarrassment, but I was getting used to it.

Hell, what was I talking about?

I had been used to being embarrassed my entire life. I was never the most graceful of people. I stepped to the side, and she hurried in, over to a large rack in the corner with several pieces of clothing hanging from it. To be honest, I hadn't even realized it was there. It could've been some stealth ninja hiding in my room that entire time and I would've just completely ignored the fact that they were there in plain sight.

She hurried back over and curtsied to me before rushing out of the room. I could tell I had scared her, which wasn't surprising since I often scared myself. As I went to close the door, several guards walked past, with Willa at the helm. They opened the door and ushered her into the room before I could even call out to her. As the door shut, her eyes met mine, but her face was completely blank and emotionless. In fact, her eyes were deep in the same brilliant color they used to be.

Willa looked straight at me, knowing what had happened in the castle, knowing my uncle had been attacked and didn't say a single word. When her door closed, two guards turned and crossed their arms over their chests, staring at me. I chuckled nervously and shut the door, locking myself back into the room. I was trying desperately not to take Willa's actions toward me to heart. There could have easily been a simple explanation, or there could've really been a complex one. Either way, I wouldn't know until I had a chance to sit down with her, and until the ball was over, that wasn't something that was going to happen. It was hard not to get my feelings hurt. Willa was basically my only family, and we had always been super close. I had never experienced a time in our relationship where she'd had anything less than an exuberant personality.

Between the dim lighting in the room and the incredible number of things that had happened that day, my mind was tired of thinking. I stretched out my arms, shuffled back toward the bed, and pulled the book from beneath the pillow. I knew there was something important about the symbol in the book, but that night I wasn't sure I could really figure out what that was. I walked around the bed to the nightstand and tucked it into the drawer.

As I walked past the window to grab my pajamas and tuck myself into bed, a shimmer of light outside caught my attention. I was just about to ignore it, based on the fact that I knew there were probably guards looking for whoever attacked my uncle, but there was something suspicious about it. I walked over to the window, hiding most of my body behind the long, thick drapes, and peeked out. I didn't see any guards anywhere. The only thing lit up besides the glow from the night garden was the small orb of light bobbing up and down, moving across the long, open field toward a cabin in the distance.

The person or being caring the light was shrouded in a dark cloak with night hiding everything except the orb. In the distance, there was a broken-down cottage, something I hadn't even noticed until that point because it was so unassuming. Who, on a night where there was possibly an attacker on the loose, would venture across the field to an old broken down cabin?

Don't do it. Just go to bed. Wait until morning and go with Shade to investigate.

My common sense tried really hard to talk me out of what I already knew I was getting ready to do. As usual, I pushed back the more practical solutions, grabbed a light-blue velvet cloak from the hanger, and slipped my feet back into my boots. I cracked open the door and glanced out, quickly pulling back and holding the door shut before the guard could see me. He seemed to be doing a check of the hallway. I waited patiently and listened, finally hearing him go back into his room and shut the door. The two guards who had been across the hall were gone, and I didn't see Shade anywhere.

As carefully and quietly as I could, I crept out of the room and down the hall, walking on my tiptoes the entire way not to make a sound on the floor. When I had finally made it around the corner, my shoulders fell, and I let out a deep breath of relief. I wasn't exactly sure why I was relieved. I was basically sending myself into a perilous situation and had no idea what to expect. I had every ability to call on Shade, Esmeralda, or even Harry. But come to think of it, I couldn't remember seeing Esmeralda or Harry since we had arrived. I had only assumed they were by Willa's side because that was basically what they had come there for. It was still kind of strange that we hadn't even crossed paths once.

Once I was in the clear, I wasn't worried about others seeing me. We had been pretty low-key with the rest of the castle, and they didn't think twice of another fae walking in or out at whatever hour they wanted to. I took one of the side balcony exits and meandered through the night air, trying to act nonchalant when a guard watch came by and wondered what I was doing. However, looking all around the grounds, I didn't see a single guard anywhere except the front gate. It was very strange, considering we had an attacker on the loose.

I pulled the hood over my head and wrapped the cloak around me as I moved away from the castle and across the open field toward the broken-down cabin. I made a circle to the right and came around, seeing the flickering light inside as I approached. Pressing myself closer to the house, I inched over to one of the windows with all the broken glass removed. I ducked down under the ledge listening to the voices inside. They were quiet, and the creaking of the house and blowing of the wind across the field was making it very hard to hear. That was probably the point. I couldn't really think of any other reason than nefarious ones for someone to meet in an old, broken-down cabin at the back end of the fae castle. They definitely were not discussing place settings for the ball the following night.

There were two voices, neither one of them particularly familiar, but not unfamiliar, either. They were monotone, and I couldn't tell gender or age from how they spoke. It wasn't like I could guess the age of the fae anyway. They may look twenty-three but actually be two thousand and thirty years old. It was very strange to me. One of the voices was all of a sudden loud, and I backed up against the house, realizing that they were right above me, looking out the window as they talked.

"The princess is under control. You don't need to worry about that."

"It's my job to worry. We need to put things in motion." The second voice was deeper, and it sent chills up my spine.

The first voice whispered with a sharp bite to their tone. "I've taken care of this just as I said I would. The princess is not going to bother anyone or be thinking for themselves anytime soon. Now, we'll have fewer eyes on us."

"Where are we on the timeline?"

The person standing above me in the open window turned away, walking back into the cottage. I rolled my eyes, my hand pressed my chest, trying not to make a sound. I could hear one of their footsteps because of the creaky wooden floors.

The first voice dipped even quieter, and I lifted my ear, trying to make out what they were saying. "We're precisely on schedule. Everything will happen on the night of the ball. We won't let anyone get in the way this time. Execute it well. And don't contact me like this again. I'd come to you if I needed you."

In an interesting play of power, the first voice had taken control of the situation and cut off any more dialogue. I crept back toward the far end of the house so I could hide as soon as they came out the front door, but no one came out. The light inside went out, and stillness fell over the cottage. Wherever they had gone, they didn't come out the front door. In the distance, closer to the castle, I could see several guards with lights flowing in front of them, searching the grounds. I needed to get back before someone knew I was gone. Since I couldn't trust anybody, I didn't want to get caught and give away my upper hand in the situation.

The ball was the next evening, and whatever was about to go down, I knew it had to do with Willa, the stone, and our lives.

18

Callie

WHEN I FINALLY MANEUVERED MYSELF like a special agent around the property of the castle and up the stairs back into the safety of the walls, or the mirage of safety that they provided, I made a beeline straight for Willa's aunt's room to let her know what I had found out.

Obviously, someone was planning something for the ball, and I needed to make sure Willa was 100% safe. I had no idea who was behind it or who was even in that cabin. In reality, I didn't even know where they went because they didn't come out the back door, and they didn't go out the front door.

I knew the fae could take care of that, though. That wasn't my job, but it might help lead us to where the stone was and maybe even Willa's father and the king of the witches. In my hurry, I wasn't paying much attention to where I was going. It wasn't like the holes were packed full of fae. It was practically the middle of the night, and not even the guards breath their normal posts. I had taken a count of every guard on the first night to know where the safety was and, if something happened, where he needed to get to. That was my whole play-it-safe tactic that I had used just about everywhere I went.

As I rounded the corner, my eyes on the prize, I ran straight into Shade, slamming into his chest. I stumbled backward, and he grabbed my arm, keeping me from falling.

I shook the impact-created daze from my head. "I'm so sorry… I…"

As my eyes reached Shade's, I realized that not only was he up in the middle of the night, which wasn't all that suspicious for Shade, but he was wearing a cloak, and it looked like he had just come from outside. His hair was windswept, and his cheeks were red. With as pale as his skin was as a fae, complexion changes were easy to spot. He followed my eyes down his cloak the back up to me. He reached out for my arm, but I stepped back, narrowing my eyes at him.

"Callie, what's wrong with you? Why are you out here, and why are you wearing a cloak?"

"I feel like I should be asking you the same question...."

I couldn't help but be suspicious. It just so happened that even though I hadn't seen Shade in the hallway when I had snuck out, and I hadn't seen him on the grounds as I was making my way to the cottage, he was outside at the same time as me? I took another step back and shook my head. "I've just got to get to Willa's aunt."

Before he could ask any questions, I hurried around him and raced down the hall as quickly as I could. I stopped as I went around the next corner, just making sure he wasn't following me. My heart was beating wildly in my chest. I couldn't tell if the tingling was from my nervousness about what I had heard at the cottage or from the fact that my mind was telling me one thing about Shade, but he was showing something completely different.

Up ahead, the sound of someone clearing their throat pulled me from my thoughts. A guard was standing in front of the queen regent's quarters, the same place I had been earlier, giving me a suspicious look. I grinned nervously and walked down, straightening myself out. "I need to speak to the queen regent right away. It's a matter of security and safety.

Before the guard could even knock on the door, the queen regent threw it open and stared at me, looking a bit frazzled. I could only assume she had been woken up either by me or by someone else. Either way, she didn't look delighted that I was standing at her door. For all intents and purposes, I wasn't happy to be standing at her door.

"Queen regent, I'm sorry to interrupt you or wake you up, but I just..." I looked back at the guard.

The queen regent waved me in. "Take a deep breath and tell me what you heard."

I waited until she closed the door before spilling the whole story without even taking a breath in between. She listened to me calmly with that normal non-expression on her face that the fae were apparently very good at and then nodded. "I know all of this already. I've already dispatched guards to track them down."

"But..."

She put her hand on my back and walked toward the door. "Trust me, Callie. I promise I'll keep everyone safe."

A wild tingle ran up my arm and across my chest, the same uncomfortable burning that I had when I first met her. Willa's aunt opened the door and pressed on my back, letting me know she was giving me more than a gentle nudge out the door. I stepped out and turned around, not even sure what I was going to say but wanting to protest her nonchalant brushoff of what I had seen, but she had already closed the door in my face. I glanced up at the guard, looking straight ahead and not paying me a bit of attention before turning and walking back to my room.

Once inside, I locked all the locks, lit a couple of candles because it was far too dark in the room for me with the way I was feeling, and climbed into bed, pulling the covers up and tightly around me. Despite the extreme comfort of the bed that night, I couldn't help but stare at the door, waiting for some sort of shadow to fall in the hallway. There were all sorts of emotions going through me, and I wasn't sure what to do with one of them. I didn't want to believe that Shade was the person responsible for everything. I didn't want to believe that he was in on the kidnappings, stealing the stone, and the King Collector.

With a cocktail of fear and sadness swirling around in me, I lay there for most of the night until I gently fell asleep right before dawn. It was the first time since Rome that I fell asleep, wondering if I would even wake up the next morning.

19

Callie

WHEN I WAS BARELY AN ADULT, I could remember standing in my parents' house, the world moving around me, the feeling as if I were standing still in time. The emotions, the commotion, and the sheer drama of my parents' death freezing me right where I was.

It had taken me a lot of time to get past that, to feel that I was moving forward with the world again. But on that day, meandering through the hallways of the castle, everyone wild and busy working on preparations for the ball that night, I was back there again.

I hadn't gone to breakfast as I didn't really want to see Shade at that moment. I knew he would ask me about the night before, and I didn't know what to tell him. Even after a good night's sleep, I still had my questions, my suspicions. Then, the queen regent seemed to be brushing me off more and more as time passed. I wanted to know how they already knew about the people in the cabin, and I wanted answers. I wasn't there for a vacation. I was there to help Willa.

Willa…

That was another thing blowing around in my head. My own best friend had turned into somebody I didn't even recognize anymore. And it wasn't her appearance. It was the fact that she had withdrawn entirely from us altogether. She hadn't checked in, she hadn't checked it on my uncle, and she had completely ignored me the last time I saw her. Something was going on, but I couldn't put my finger on it. There were too many missing chunks of the story to get anywhere close to understanding what was happening.

There was nothing really for me to do for several hours before it was time to get ready for the ball, so I headed over to see my uncle and find out how he was doing. I had received a message that morning from one of the server girls letting me know that my uncle was awake. I was hoping he had some more insight into who had attacked them.

I barely knew the man at all, but when I walked into his room, which oddly looked a lot like a hospital, the smile on his face made all the anxiety flutter away, at least for a little while. "Look at you! Sitting up and everything! How are you feeling?"

Alabaster grinned, finishing up the last bite of the food that had been brought for him. He may have been awake, but he still looked pretty rough. The bruising and swelling had gone out a bit, and the magic that the fae were using to heal him seemed to be working, but I could tell he wasn't anywhere near ready for what I feared was coming. I also knew I couldn't really talk to him about it because he was a finder. He wouldn't be able to tell me anything useful, and it would just take away from his ability to have a nice conversation with me. Not to mention, he needed to rest. I didn't want him attempting to get up before he was ready just because I had overheard a conversation that may or may not have been concerning. I had suspicions about someone who was, unfortunately, leading the charge on everything, but he couldn't help in the shape he was in.

"I think I've seen better days, but I'm alive. I shook my head. "We've all been terrified. Do you remember anything about who attacked you?"

He shook his head. "I remember there was a noise, and then I remember waking up here. They're hoping I get my memory back soon, and I do, too, because whoever did this is going to be really sorry when I get a hold of them."

It was hard to take him seriously looking the way he did, but there was no doubt in my mind that my uncle had some sort of mean streak in him. The kind that he only pulled out for the most well-deserving of people, and whoever did that to him was definitely well-deserving.

He stared at me for a moment and then smiled. "You look like your mother."

That was always the best compliment ever. "You met my mother?"

He nodded, pushing the tray away from him. "Just once, but I'll never forget it. I was going through a rather lonely time with no family or friends, stuck on Earth, when I decided to look up your mother. I knew I couldn't just walk into her life and try to explain everything, so I went to her house is as a solicitor for the church."

I wrinkled my nose. "I'm sure she loved that. I'm surprised you even got to talk to her."

He began to laugh and reached up, wincing as he gripped his side. "She was definitely fiery. She let down her guard pretty quickly, though, when she realized that I had just as much of a fiery personality as her. She offered me some coffee, and we sat and talked for several hours. She looked so much like my family, with the creases next to her eyes and the laugh lines because she was always smiling. It was right after I heard that your parents had gotten married, and I know they didn't have you that long after that, so she may have been pregnant with you at the time."

It warmed my heart to hear the story. Not only did I rarely hear stories about my mother that I hadn't heard before, but it made me remember things about her that I had all but forgotten. Things like the lines at the edge of her eyes or the way she always smiled. But that happiness didn't last as long as I wanted it to. The events of the night and what I had heard were weighing on me heavily.

Alabaster reached up and touched my arm.

"What's going on? I can see it all on your face. Did something happen?"

I hesitated for a moment, not wanting to tell them. Still, my uncle gave me a look so similar to the one my mother used to give me when I didn't want to tell her the truth about something that I couldn't help but fess up. Suffice it to say, he wasn't too thrilled about the fact that I went out following these people to the abandoned cabin without letting anybody know. It wasn't like I was a child, though. I felt like in the fae world, they treated me like that. I was an adult, and I made a decision, and I was glad I had. I just wasn't sure what to do with it at that point.

He gripped tighter to my wrist as I told the story, and when I was done, he took a long, deep breath and sat up farther in the bed. "I need you to be careful. I need you to be watchful during the ball."

"Telling Callie some of your riddles?" Shade asked with a chuckle as he walked into the room.

I tried not to visibly flinch at the sound of his voice, but it was really hard after seeing him the night before. I watched as he lovingly greeted Alabaster and then pulled up a chair next to the bed. Alabaster shook his head, and I knew it was coming. He launched right into how we needed to be safe and secure after what had happened the night before, and I could see the confusion riddled on Shade's face.

"You don't know?"

"I just haven't had a chance to tell them," I interjected.

Reluctantly, I told him the story as fast as I could, trying to ignore the glares of anger he was throwing in my direction. I was glad he chose not to reprimand me or want to have a conversation right there in front of Alabaster.

Instead, he paused for a moment and then nodded. "I agree that we should be watchful but inconspicuous. We want to blend in so nobody notices us. If somebody is watching us, they'll still think we know nothing about it or have no suspicions whatsoever."

I quickly stood up, wanting to leave before Shade so that I could avoid the conversation altogether. "Well, Uncle, I'll come back to see you, but I've gotta go get ready for the ball. Apparently, there's a team there ready and waiting for me."

Shade went to stand up. "I can walk you out."

I waved my hands. "No need. My uncle needs you more than I do. I'll see you tonight."

I tucked my tail and ran as fast as possible, hoping Shade didn't follow me. Thankfully, he did not. I kept moving through as quickly as I could back to my room. The truth was, it wasn't time for me to get ready yet, but I just wanted out of that situation. No matter how nice Shade seemed, I fought with my suspicions against him, coupled with my desire to kiss him. It was miserable, and the last thing I wanted was for him to suck me back in. If I were going to be inconspicuous, I would be inconspicuous with him as well.

When I arrived at my room, I paused and decided that maybe I should try to talk to Willa. I was sure she was probably nervous about the ball, and it might give me a chance to gauge what she knew and what she didn't. However, as I walked up to the door, one of the guards stepped in my way. "We're sorry, but she isn't to be disturbed."

My brow wrinkled. "I'm pretty sure if you tell her it's me, shall be fine with it."

The guard shook his head. "I'm sorry, we were given strict orders."

I looked at the door and them, in my mind contemplating whether I could pull some amazing stunt move and slide between their legs, simultaneously opening the door and rushing into Willa's room. Then reality slapped me, and I knew that I'd just end up probably banging my forehead against one of their crotches and knocking myself out, heading to the ball with a black eye. That wasn't a story I wanted to tell. So, with that unsettled feeling in my stomach, I went back into my room and sat on the edge of the bed. I would just wait there until it was time to get ready to face whatever was headed my way.

As I sat there on the edge of the mattress, my bracelet was buzzing wildly. It hadn't stopped since I had gone to see the queen regent, and it was getting stronger by the second. Some points almost took my breath away. It was as if the magic were trying to tell me something. But I wasn't a magical being, so understanding it was virtually impossible for me. All I knew was that it was incredibly uncomfortable and whatever it was trying to relay to me wasn't something I could ignore. There was nothing I could do about it, though. So, for now, I focused on what I would do to blend into the ball and keep my eyes peeled for anyone suspicious. If they hadn't caught the person in the cabin and they were still out there, the plan was still in motion.

If the plan were still in motion… Well, I might just want to wear my yoga pants under my dress in case I had to make a mad dash.

20

Shade

MELODIC MUSIC PLAYED QUIETLY in the background as fae from all over the realm gathered in their most beautiful dresses and fae suits to mingle and celebrate the return of Princess Willa.

It was an extraordinarily glamorous event, far beyond anything in the human world. Magic transformed the ceiling into a sparkling diamond sky. Vines moved and blossomed along the walls, and pixies carried trays of drinks with their wings fluttering in overtime. Tables were sectioned out and spaced, strategically planned for who would sit where. They explained the ball as the re-welcoming of the princess for the people, but none of the real people of the fae realm were actually there.

Much like on Earth, those kinds of affairs only included those of the highest caliber and status. Beneath my magical exterior, I was not one of those people. However, I wasn't there for the pomp and circumstance. I was there to help find the stone, the fae king, and most importantly, my brother.

I wouldn't lie and say that Callie wasn't another reason I didn't hesitate to cross realms. Ever since I had run into her the night before, she had been acting strange. While I wanted to know what was going on, it was not the time.

There was a threat, not just the underlying danger of the King Collector, but a significant threat that none of us were very sure was being taken seriously by Willa's aunt, who up until that night was the queen regent. Willa would take that spot, though I wasn't sure exactly how that would work if she were trying to find the stone and her father at the same time. I hadn't seen Willa's face since we had arrived, and I had no idea where Esmeralda or Harry had gone. They had to take care of themselves at some point, and I had to focus on finding my brother and keeping Callie safe.

That night we were going to be unassuming, fading into the background and watching just as the guards did all throughout the days and nights of the fae castle. I kept my eyes open for Callie, waiting for her to arrive. I knew that she wasn't looking forward to a formal event, which made two of us. I not only hated the stuffy-shirt act that I had to put on for all the important people, but there were far more important things to think about than rubbing elbows with high society. We weren't in my home, though, and I didn't have a lot of control over what happened.

A small murmur fell over the crowd, but they continued talking. I glanced around the room, my eyes falling on a beautiful woman entering on the arm of one of the servants whose job it was to walk in anyone who was not accompanied by a date. The woman was breathtaking, and it took me at least two minutes before I realized who I was looking at.

Callie stood in the entryway of the ballroom with her hair pinned up loosely, flowers decorating it like a crown. She wasn't wearing a large puff-sleeve gown like she thought she was going to. That was just a little tease from Willa. Instead, she wore a thin-strapped dress that sparkled like the magical ceiling and perfectly matched her skin tone. Had it not been for the floor-length skirt that hugged her curves like it was made for it, I would've thought she had just painted glitter on her body before she came. Her makeup was subtle yet beautiful against the porcelain of her skin. The only thing that threw me off was the color of her eyes.

The fae had transformed her into one of them, but her eyes were much more striking in her human form in reality. I couldn't help but smile at her, and I didn't fault myself for that as I walked across the ballroom and put my arm out for her. The servant and I nodded at each other as he transferred her arm to mine. The volume of the music raised, and several people walked out onto the dance floor. She followed my lead, and I took her hand in mine, placing my other hand on the small of her back as we readied to dance. It wasn't my initial thought, but it only seemed natural to lead her out there.

"I thought we were going to be unassuming and inconspicuous," I said, whispering in her ear as I pulled her closer to me.

She smiled, and her cheeks grew rosy. "I didn't pick this out. Blame the fae."

I leaned in, brushing my cheek against hers. "You look beautiful."

It was hard to keep my mind on the task at hand with her dancing in my arms, and for a moment, I gave in. I twirled her around the dance floor and pulled her close, looking into her eyes and having that one moment, even if it only lasted for that moment, that we had wanted to have since we met. When the song came to an end, I dipped her back. I then cleared the floor with her, standing at the edges and clapping as the royal court maneuvered into position for their traditional dance.

Glancing over at Callie, I saw her staring up at Willa. Willa sat stone straight, her eyes focused somewhere we couldn't see, her expression transfixed. Callie's eyes were sad. "She's acting so strange. It's like she's not even there anymore."

"I don't know what it is, but something's not right. We're going to get to the bottom of this." I really hoped I wasn't giving Callie false hope.

Callie

"Dammit," Shade said, standing next to me as we watched the royal court finished their dance.

"What is it?" I asked him.

He patted the front of his jacket and reached into the pockets. "I forgot something. Will you be all right here for just a moment?"

I looked around at all the fae and shrugged. "Most likely. But don't be gone too long. I might be swept away by one of these rich fae socialites."

He smirked and hurried off. I watched him until he left the room, my smile quickly fading. I moved to the outer edges of the party, holding a glass of something bubbly but not drinking it. Meandering around the crowd, I looked at every face, eventually landing myself at the entrance, leaning against the wall, waiting for Shade to return. He said he would only be gone for a moment, but that moment had quickly passed and had been quite a while. I looked up for Willa but saw that her seat was empty. That wasn't fair. If I had to be there, so did she. They probably had her taking a break or changing clothes, or whatever it was that the fae did.

The longer I was there, in the fae world, the more I wanted to go home. I was starting to feel like I was stuck in one of those fantasy movies, with no control over anything and no idea who anybody was. Anybody could be an enemy. I had no way to spot them. Frustrated, I turned from the crowd and looked out over the gardens, a few people were milling around, but it was mostly empty. Everyone was inside, rubbing elbows with each other, talking about how important they were in the fae realm.

As I scanned the scenery, I stopped, staring at a figure in the distance. I stepped out of the ball-room and onto the veranda, trying to get a closer look. The person was cloaked just like the one in my dream, and they hurried along nervously, looking around as they went. Up in the sky, magical fireworks cracked loudly above, shaking me to my core. The person hurrying along the field toward the old, abandoned cabin looked to be frightened, too. When they turned and looked back at the castle, I almost dropped my glass of bubbly.

I set it down on the table and took several steps closer, my mouth falling open. "Willa?"

Before I could get to the bottom of the steps, she had disappeared into the cabin. I hurried after her, this time not caring whether someone saw me or not. There were no guards and no one watching her. I didn't understand what was going on. I raced across the field to the cabin and found the door wide open. Carefully I stepped inside, looking around. "Willa? Are you in here?"

The place was abandoned and falling down, but in the center of the room was a hatch sitting open. I hovered over it, looking down into the darkness below. Next to the hatch were fresh footprints. I puffed out my cheeks and shook my head. "Guess it's time for another adventure."

The magic was pumping from my bracelet throughout my whole body, sending tingles of electric shock from head to toe. I turned around and carefully began to climb down the ladder, trying to ignore the fear of what I was going to stick my hands into as I went down. I really hated spiders. The climb down was farther than I thought, and the darkness made it hard to see where the bottom actually was. Taking another step down, my foot slipped, and there was a crack, the bottom of the ladder crumbling beneath me. My hands, cold and clammy from fear, released the last rung, and I fell, trying not to scream. I imagined I would fall for quite a while before I reached my untimely death, my body at the bottom of some pit where no one would ever find it. But about two seconds into the fall, I hit the ground with a thud. I was pretty much all the way to the bottom when the latter broke.

I groaned and picked myself up, a large chunk of my updo uncurling, letting strands of hair fall all over the place. My hands were darkened with dirt and soot. I shrugged and brushed them down the front of my dress, figuring, at that point, it was a lost cause anyway. I put my hand out, squinting through the cavernous space, and tried to make my way down what looked to be a hallway of sorts.

Keeping my ears perked for sounds of anyone coming in my direction, I moved as quickly as possible without making too much noise. Willa, or whoever was in that cloak, wasn't anywhere to be found, but there was no way they could've gone anywhere other than down. Up ahead, the tunnel turned to the right, and I could see the flickering light coming from around the corner. As I approached, I heard voices, and I instantly backed into the shadows.

Putting my hands down to feel behind me, I continued backing up, looking for the wall. However, when my hands finally found something, it wasn't the hard surface I expected. Instead, I felt a soft fabric with a body beneath it. Before I could even move, an arm wrapped around my chest and the other slapped a hand over my mouth, pulling me farther back into the shadows.

22

Callie

MY EYES WERE WIDE as I stood there, not knowing what to do.

If I screamed out or struggled, whoever was in the cave would hear me, and I wasn't sure I wanted them to know I was there. On the other hand, if I didn't, whoever had me pinned up against them, could easily dispose of me in three seconds without anyone ever knowing.

Contemplating my options, the voices grew fainter as if they were heading deeper into the caves. When I could no longer hear them, the hand released my mouth, and I pushed off, quickly turning around. I backed to the other side of the cave hallway and watched as someone emerged from the shadows.

"Shade? So, I was right. You are involved!" I lunged at him, slapping him hard on the chest over and over again.

Okay, it wasn't my finest moment, but he quickly grabbed my wrists and stopped me.

"Be a little bit quieter. And what are you talking about? I'm not part of this."

I put my hands on my hips, narrowing my eyes at him. "Oh yeah? And where had you gone yesterday when I came back into the castle after someone mysteriously disappeared from the cabin and I found you in your cloak having been outside? And I thought you went to your room to get something."

He stared at me for several moments with an uneasy look on his face.

I crossed my arms over my chest and lifted both eyebrows, waiting for his response. "Well?"

He untied the tie at the top of his cloak and pulled both sides open like a back alley watch salesman. However, instead of stolen goods, there were small intricately braided stems with beautiful blossoms of flowers on them. I was so confused.

Shade closed his cloak again. "I was making a small flower corsage. I know it's stupid, but it's the way the witches do things. Last night, I went out to scout the greenhouse the fae have on the property. Willa's uncle said I could pick some flowers there to make it. I ran out of time earlier and couldn't put it all together so, I wanted to do it really fast and bring it to you."

Slowly, my arms unfolded, and my shoulders relaxed though my pride took a huge hit. I felt like a complete asshole. "I... How did you end up out here?"

"Probably the same way you did. I was on my way back, and I swear I thought I saw..."

I finished the sentence "Willa?"

He nodded. "We're already down here. But we're not the only ones. I had seen several figures going in and out of the house, but I couldn't make out from a distance what kind of creatures they were."

Suddenly, the vibration of my bracelet shot up my arm, and I put my hand over it, wincing. "I think the stone has to be close. I noticed it last night when I got close to this building. The magic coming from my bracelet is almost hard to take. I think it increases the closer I get to the stone."

Shade nodded. "That makes sense. It's got a piece of that stone in it. You're like a homing beacon."

"I've been called worse." I chuckled. "Well, I think we should go after them. If that was Willa, I can't imagine that she knows what she's doing. We have to stop them and get the stone back as well as Willa. I don't know if this has anything to do with the King Collector, but if we don't do something, I feel none of us will get back to Earth. And I'll be honest with you, I really don't want to stay here."

Shade chuckled, putting his hand out to help me step down from the rock I had climbed up on. "Is the magic wearing off on you. A little too fantastical for your taste?"

I rolled my eyes and leaned my head back. "It's like being stuck in Toon Town, only there's no cute rabbits or sexy red dresses."

We both got our bearings and continued down the path, following it for quite a while. The stone beneath me was slick and wet. I kept catching my dress on short pieces of rocks or under my feet as I slipped. I was covered in dirt, and the dress, unless they had some sort of magical cleaning products, was destined for the incinerator when I was done. I just hoped that I wasn't wearing it when that happened.

I stumbled over another rock, but this time instead of catching myself, I found Shade grabbing my elbows. When I looked up at him, he had one finger to his lips and then pointed over his shoulder. At the end of the hall was an arched doorway and light coming from inside. It was dim, flickering candlelight, and the shadows danced along the walls creating a series of shadows that chilled me to my core. It almost looked as if they were real spirits guarding the entrance to wherever we were going.

Shade and I moved to the doorway and peeked in, trying to keep ourselves from being seen just yet. I immediately slapped my hand over my mouth, attempting to hold back the shock when my eyes fell on at least ten of the red-eyed creatures that had taken me before, floating around the space. In the center of the cave was the cloaked woman standing in front of a pillar that held a glowing aqua stone. The energy pulsed in the stone, and I could feel it in the piece on my wrist.

A voice echoed out from the shadows, deep and dark. I immediately stood up and pressed my back to the wall, hiding out of sight. Shade looked at me inquisitively. I closed my eyes for a second, swallowing hard, not realizing I would have such a shocked reaction. But the voice belonged to only one, a being I knew to be cruel and ruthless and also a kidnapper.

The whisper escaped my lips before I could even think. "My God, it's the King Collector."

Shade quickly shifted over to my side and stood next to me, covering my mouth and holding me close as I tried to push away the fear. The magic pulsing was so heavy that it was like having a second heartbeat. My vision was getting blurrier by the second. I felt like the magic was building up inside of me but had no way out. I wasn't meant to have that. I was just a human. Inside the cave, the King Collector began to talk to the cloaked figure.

"You have the stone, but did you bring the other part?" The King Collector bellowed.

The cloaked figure nodded and reached into its pocket, pulling out a golden chain with the same knot from the book dangling from the end of it. Shade looked at me wildly. "I know that knot. That's the symbol or the crest of the fae royalty. He pointed down at my bracelet, and I finally realized where I had seen the symbols before. I would've slapped myself in the forehead if I didn't think it would've given us a way to the King Collector inside.

"Why do they need it?" I whispered.

"Because the stone will only work with the fae, and that necklace most likely has a part of the fae royalty magic line in it."

"Good," the King Collector purred. "You've done very well. It is time for the next step."

The cloaked figure set the necklace down next to the stone and reached up, slowly pulling its hood back. As soon as it revealed Willa beneath, I shook my head defiantly. My teeth clenched, and my fists balled as I stepped from behind the wall and walked toward them. "Not today, not my best friend."

I could hear Shade hissing from behind me to stop, but I wasn't going to let Willa be taken, especially since I knew for a fact it was not by her own will. As soon as the King Collector saw me, he began to laugh maniacally, the deep sounds ricocheting off the cavern walls. Willa turned toward me, too, magic flowing down her arms and twisting around her palms. She was staring at me with pure hatred.

I shook my head and ran up to her, grabbing her face in my hands. "Willa, this is not you.

You're under some sort of spell. Fight it. Don't let this take you over. This is not who you are."

Shade ran up. "Callie, don't do it. That's not Willa."

My head snapped toward him, and I angrily glared. "What do you mean it's not Willa? I know my best friend. I just have to break whatever spell she's under."

Shade shook his head, but before he could speak again, Willa began to laugh, and her laughter began to change. Slowly, I looked back at her finding myself staring straight into her aunt's eyes, the former queen regent. "What the…"

I dropped my hands and took a step back, but her aunt was on me before I could get away. Her arm snapped out, and she grabbed my neck, lifting me into the air. Shade made a movement to pull his magic, but the dark-cloaked figures with red eyes swooped in, dragging him back and stifling his magic. I looked down at Willa's aunt's face, feeling her hand tighten around my neck. Her laughter began to fade, and she looked over toward the shadows.

"We've met before. Take the bracelet, dispose of the girl."

She smiled nefariously as she slowly lowered my feet back down to the ground. She released my neck, but before I could move, she grabbed my arm, dragging me toward the stone.

I shook my head. "You'll have to cut off my arm because this thing is not coming off. Trust me, I've tried. Besides, I'm not really in the mood for letting you borrow it."

She tilted her head to the side, staring at me for a moment before lifting her hands, dark violet magic spiraling up and outward. As it moved, it revealed the handle and that the blade of the sword. She lifted my arm and yanked me over, pinning it down next to stone on the pedestal. Strong straps of magic appeared, tightening down over my forearm and keeping me in place. Willa's aunt turned the sword back and forth, smiling. "I guess we'll just have to cut it off then."

"No!" Shade yelled, still fighting off the dark spirits attacking him.

I tried to move or pull away, to do anything, but the straps held me firmly in place. I looked up at Willa's aunt. "Why?"

Her aunt paused for just a moment and looked at me. "Because I'm the fae queen, and I have a right to the throne. If we possess the stone and the sister stone, we will be unstoppable."

With that, a smile moved back across her lips, and she pulled the sword back, ready to strike. I clenched my eyes shut and tensed my whole body, knowing there was no way I could get out of it. Something was telling me, cutting off my arm was only the beginning. I was going to die in there, and it wouldn't be a quick death.

23

Callie

I TRIED to take myself to another world without feeling the magical blade come down on my flesh.

I didn't allow my body to quake or shake in fear. I stood resolute in the finality of her swing. However, after waiting and waiting... and waiting, I finally opened one eye to see what was taking so long. Either she was ruthless, or she had changed her mind.

But it seemed that it was neither. Magic was flowing in the same color as hers from my bracelet to her sword. It was wrapped around, intertwined with her own, fighting Willa's aunt away from me. With one strong surge, it ripped the sword right out of her hand and shattered the magic bindings around my wrist. I lifted my hand and rubbed the skin, all the fear immediately leaving my body. Something was happening. It felt as if small orbs of magic began bursting all over my body. I felt strong, brave, and powerful. It was as if the magic itself was moving me. It was taking me over and protecting me.

Without much cognizance to my own movements, my arms began thrusting back and forth, sending strikes of magic straight at Willa's aunt. It looked as if the magic was exactly the same as she was using, only it seemed to overpower hers so easily. I took a step forward and then another, and another, backing Willa's aunt up into the corner as I struck her relentlessly with bolts of magic.

She gritted her teeth and looked straight at me, screaming at the top of her lungs. She waved her arms up and around and then vanished into thin air. Immediately, my magic stopped and my arms dropped. The sound of Shade fighting the red-eyed creatures turned me toward him. I put my hands up with my magic racing, wanting so badly to be released. However, before I could attack and help Shade, the King Collector called out for me.

"Wait! Why would you want to kill my creatures when it means you'll be killing one of your own?"

Confused, I turned toward the shadows. "One of my own? These red-eyed beasts are not mine."

"But that's not what I'm talking about. You wouldn't want to sacrifice your sweet friend's beloved uncle, would you?"

The shadows twisted, and Willa's uncle, Bailey, came stumbling out, falling to his knees. His hands were bound by magic, and he was gagged with it as well. He shook his head at me, but I closed my eyes, finding that the situation was exactly what I wanted to avoid.

"What do you want?"

"That's easy. I want you. I want you to join my army. I will trade you for him."

Shade protested from behind me, and Uncle Bailey grunted, shaking his head. I turned my sight from them to the dark shadows. I knew just how important Willa's uncle was to her. Even more, with the aunt gone, Willa's uncle was the only other one who could take on the role of running the kingdom. I knew that Willa did not want to be the queen regent. She would have no choice if I left her uncle there to die. I knew what it was like to lose family, people I loved who were very close to me. I couldn't be the cause of that for my best friend."

The magic pulled back into my palms, and I took another step forward. "Fine, but both he and Shade are allowed to leave here unscathed. You will not hunt them or try to find them. And the same goes for Willa."

"No, Callie, you can't trust his word. He'll betray you immediately," Shade yelled.

I knew he was right, but I also knew I couldn't make any other choice. I took a deep breath and stepped closer, putting out both of my arms. The King Collector began to chuckle deeply, letting out a satisfied sigh of victory. The dark ropes around Uncle Bailey's wrists fell away, and so did the gag in his mouth. He tried to run up to me, shaking his head.

"Don't do this. You don't need to do this."

The King Collector roared and used his magic to throw Uncle Bailey straight at Shade. As soon as he did, the shadows curled out, clamping down on both of my wrists. It burned, and my magic wailed and screamed inside of me. I had never felt anything like that before. It was as if it were entering me, killing every bit of my magic on its way. As it began to envelop me, I screamed out, falling to my knees. The bracelet was desperately trying to fight it, but it was just too much. I had made my choice, and I hoped that at least getting Willa's aunt out of the picture would open up an opportunity for the rest of them to defeat the King Collector and save the realms. If that was my contribution, my life, then I wouldn't hesitate.

The magic moved up to my elbows and began to swirl around my upper arms toward my shoulders. Suddenly, a pure bright flash of white light lit up the room so bright I couldn't see anything but the light. It was only for a moment, but it was enough to strike back against the darkness. I could feel it retreat, pulling back, hissing in recoil.

I looked over my shoulder, my vision blurry and the room slightly spinning.

Willa was standing in her dress, wearing a pair of tennis shoes, with Esmeralda and Harry behind her on either side. She shook her head. "I don't think so, boss. You crashed this party, and I think it's time for you to leave."

Willa didn't even hesitate, and neither did Esmeralda and Harry. They began to move their bodies back and forth, swinging their arms. Wild waves of magic raced out of them, speeding around the room, encircling the shadows. I had never seen Willa do full-on magic before, but the way she spun her hands and twisted her own powers was like a dance. And it was one hell of a dance, too. Within seconds the darkness moved completely away, the last bit of it retreating in fear. A calming, soothing warmth washed over me. I wasn't sure if it was the bracelet or Willa, but I appreciated it.

Willa looked over at me and gave me a grin. "Callie, Shade, get down!"

We both dropped to the ground. I pressed my cheek against the cool stone as Willa mustered an enormous moving orb of energy. She lifted it to the top of the cave, and when she had it at the perfect position, she thrust her arms outward and back, splitting the orb. Magic shot out like lightning bolts, striking everything around us. The dark shadows receded, and I could hear the King Collector screeching in anger until it finally disappeared.

Willa, Esmeralda, and Harry chased off the last of the few red-eyed creatures as I slowly picked myself up off the ground. Willa walked over to me and looked me up and down. "If you didn't want to wear a dress that bad, you could've just told me."

I stared at Willa silently for several moments, tears filling my eyes. I had never been so happy to see Willa in my life. I lunged at her and wrapped my arms around her, hugging her tightly.

She leaned in and hugged me back, and I knew that whatever had happened, my best friend was back. "You run off during my ball, trade your life for my uncle's, make sure that my realm and people who aren't even yours are safe... What am I going to do with you?"

I sniffled and pulled back, wiping the tears from my cheeks. "A nice long vacation on a private island with alcohol and pool boys is a good start."

Callie

THE BELLS RINGING at the fae castle echoed across the land and out to the ocean beyond.

It was a beautiful day in the fae realm, pretty much like every other day in the fae realm. The coronation of the royal member to take over during the king's absence was done, and I stood at the edge of the bluffs, looking out over the water, dreaming of home.

"This is what oceans look like when humans don't turn them into trash pits," Willa said, walking up next to me.

"Yeah, except our serial killers aren't super-human creatures from another realm. You could totally just stab one in the eye and they die."

Willa looked out over the water. "Touché."

I took a deep breath and clapped my hands. "Are you sad to leave?"

Willa shrugged. "A little, but I'm really glad to get back to my life. And besides, we can't stay here forever, and if I'm going to find my father and the witch king, I need to be where I know we're all safe and you don't have to walk around in disguise."

"Personally, I kind of like the instant facelift, but I'm pretty sure Shade is going to kill someone if he doesn't get his long hair and black makeup back."

"I heard that," Shade yelled from a distance.

We both looked over at him, standing with Esmeralda, Harry, Bailey, and Alabaster. I put my arm around Willa and shook my head. "This was definitely more of an adventure than my time in Rome. I just don't understand what happened. I don't understand magic, and I don't know all the spells and the trickery. All I know is I saw your face, and it changed into your aunt's face, and she tried to cut off my arm."

Willa winced. "I never liked her. She wanted

to be queen, she wanted power, and she thought she could do it to the King Collector. She was going to pin the whole thing on me so she could claim she did it for the kingdom when she killed me. She put a fae charm on me. It was like I was trapped in my body, and I could see some of what was going on, but I couldn't communicate, and I was basically programmed."

"Yeah, I didn't really like robot Willa. You were kind of a bitch."

"I learned from the best," she said, giggling and poking me in the side.

I rolled my eyes as we walked over toward the others. Uncle Bailey stood with his king regent shawl on and crown and put his arms out toward Willa.

She ran into them and hugged him tightly. "Thank you for looking after the realm for me. I'll never find Father if I have to be queen regent. And I think that the witch king's brother has proven to us enough loyalty on numerous occasions that is just as important to find his brother as well."

Bailey glanced over at Shade, who stood quietly, waiting for his reply. Bailey smiled. "I agree. And when all of this is said and done, and we have your father firmly back on the throne, I'm going to recommend that we end the separation between witches and fae. I know it'll be rocky, but this could be a new beginning for all of us. Then you can come to visit more often."

Willa chuckled. "And you can come to visit me, too."

I turned to Alabaster, who looked a lot better. It seemed that Willa wasn't the only one under a fae charm. As soon as her aunt was gone, Alabaster remembered everything. He had been in the library that day when she had attacked him. She had frozen his memories so he couldn't remember and had kept him injured and sick. He was better within two days after she was gone.

"Are you sure you don't want to come back to Earth?"

Alabaster laughed. "No, I think being back home is good for me. But I am thankful that I met some of my family. It's been a very long and lonely time by myself. And King Bailey has asked me to work with him and the guard. It's a fresh start for all of us."

Giving in, I leaned forward and hugged him, feeling his hesitation at first but then finding that he leaned into it and hugged me back. "I'm always here. And I'm glad that I don't have to be alone anymore, either. I'm sure we'll see each other again soon. Hopefully, we have the king with us."

"Are you ready?" Harry asked.

I turned, furrowed my brow, and put my hands on my hips. "Where exactly were the two of you the whole time?"

Esmeralda had already changed back into the older lady with wild hair and a cat sweater. "In the dungeons. We didn't even get a fae charm. We just got yanked from our beds in the middle of the night and thrown in the dungeons."

I grimaced. "I'm sorry. If I had known, I would've absolutely come to look for you."

Esmeralda waved her hands. "It's all right. I'm actually pretty glad to go back. My loyalties are with Princess Willa, and I miss my cats."

"I have to finish my novel," Harry replied.

Willa nudged Shade. "You sure you don't want to go back as a fae? I can make it happen."

"I've never been more sure about anything in my life," he said in a monotone voice.

As the portal began to open, the air was filled with laughter, and I looked back at Alabaster, who gave me a nod and a wink. I hoped that in the end, when everything was set right, I'd be able to come back to the fae realm and visit. But as I looked through the portal, seeing my living room on the other side with my cat and dog waiting for me, I had never been so happy to cross realms in my life. Sure, adventure was good for me, but I was ready for some peace and quiet.

We all stepped through the portal one at a time, with Shade the last as usual, bringing up the rear. I turned and watched the portal close, seeing Alabaster bowing to me until the wall between realms was closed.

"Bloody hell, you survived," Mr. Hobbles said, popping up on the back of the couch to rub himself against my face. "The service has been subpar since you've been gone. I was beginning to fear for my safety. You have returned just in the nick of time."

I chuckled and rubbed his head. "I missed you, too. You would've hated the fae realm. Evil overlords attempted to remove limbs, and I completely destroyed a formal dress."

Mr. Hobbles shook his head. "The horror. You poor thing. If I had thumbs, I'd draw you a bath immediately."

I laughed, looking around the place. The others were at the coffee shop, and Willa had already texted them to let them know we were back. The house was way cleaner than what we had left it, which I appreciated, but I knew they didn't do it for me. They did it so that they didn't have to wear an entire sweater made from cat and dog hair out of the house every day. It would only take the cat and dog about three hours to get it back to the way it was.

"Well, I'm on my way to get my cats," Esmeralda said, kissing Willa on the cheek. "Call me if you need me."

Harry bowed to Willa, and they turned, heading out of the house. Willa put both arms out to the side and took a deep breath. "Home sweet home. Well, kind of. Your home sweet home, but it's just the same." She looked at Shade. "Thank you. I know that we didn't find your brother, but I think we've gotten one step closer. And thank you for looking out for my best friend and for me and my realm. It was beyond anything you were required to do. It definitely will be remembered. Are you staying for dinner?"

Shade glanced at me but shook his head. "No, I need to get back to Rome and check on everything there to make sure nothing caught on fire or burned down while I was gone. But I will be back soon. More often than I was before because I think we need to put our heads together in order to find your father and my brother."

Willa nodded and patted him on the arm,

watching as he and I exchanged awkward glances. She swung her arms back and forth and began to giggle. "I'm just gonna get a glass of water and let you two say goodbye."

I shot her a nasty look but then smiled at Shade when I turned back. There was an awkward moment with shuffling of feet and limbs swinging before we finally hugged each other. I closed my eyes for a moment, knowing that it would be a while before I could hug him again. I would take closeness with him over dreaming of him any day. Before I pulled back, I whispered into his ear, "Thank you for being there. Thank you for being inconspicuous and for saving me in the caves."

We pulled back, and he shook his head. "I didn't save you. You are more than capable. And it looks as if the magic and that bracelet are starting to work better with you. You might not want to give it up by the end of it."

I rolled my eyes and shook my head. "Not a chance. It will be really nice when I don't have to constantly feel like I have electrical bolts jolting through my body. Or the build-up until they just take over and explode from me. But at least I got the opportunity. Will you be back soon?"

He looked at his watch. "Hopefully. But you

know how to get a hold of me if anything happens."

I nodded, and there were another couple of moments of awkwardness where I wasn't sure whether he was going to hug me again, kiss me, or run off screaming.

He turned to leave, and I called out for him.

"Can I ask you a question?"

He shifted his eyes back and forth. "Sure."

I pursed my lips, just making sure I wanted to ask. "You don't by chance happen to fly, do you? Like maybe on a broomstick?"

He blinked at me dramatically several times before shaking his head. Right before he disappeared, teleporting back to Rome, I could hear his laugh echo out. At least he didn't take it bad.

I stood there in the silence for several seconds, then rolled my eyes, turning toward the kitchen. "Okay, come out."

Willa peeked around the corner, and right below her, Mr. Hobbles did, too. "Were you both eavesdropping?"

Willa shrugged, plopping down on the couch. Mr. Hobbles jumped up next to her and sat. "You should just tell him how you feel, Callie. It's not like you don't deserve a little love."

"I would have to agree with her," the cat

replied. "It pains me to say that, but sometimes she's not a complete moron."

Willa gasped and leaned down, grabbing Mr. Hobbles and pulling him into her. "Awe, I love you, too."

"Human! Put me down immediately. See what I mean? You give them an inch, and they'll smother you to death in their human flesh. I'm sorry, fae flesh."

I laughed and shook my head, watching as Mr. Hobbles jumped down and hurried off down the hall. As he passed the still sleeping dog, he took a swipe at him and raced off. Bean snorted awake and looked around but then quickly went back to sleep. I plopped down onto the couch next to Willa and leaned my head against her shoulder.

"It looks really clean in here," Willa whispered. "Like hospital clean."

I nodded. "It's nice. Remember what it looks like because it'll probably never look like this again."

The silence of my house had never felt better. Of course, as soon as I started to relax…weirdness ensued. Suddenly, echoing like from an intercom throughout my entire house was a loud, deep moan.

I sat straight up, and Willa jumped to her feet.

I glanced back and forth in the room then up at Willa. "What the hell was that?"

The sound echoed out again. I jumped to my feet, grabbing Willa's arm.

She shook her head, her eyes wide. "Oh no. That's not a good sign."

I was clinging to her, unsure of whether I should be curious of who had moved into my attic or worried that I would become possessed. "What's not a good sign? The moaning woman or the fact that I didn't make that up, and it's actually a poltergeist in my house ready to suck me into the static on the television?"

Willa shook her head very slowly. "That's no poltergeist... It looks like you have a new room-mate... One that carries a message that I don't think you want."

I turned and looked at her, narrowing my eyes. "What message?"

Willa gripped my hand tightly and met my eyes. "Death." She leaned in and lowered her voice to a whisper. "There's a Banshee in here."

I was starting to want the portal to the fae world back.

Whoever she was, I hope she liked coffee and yoga pants...

GRAB BOOK 3!

Loving the Story? Grab Book 3!

THANK YOU FOR READING!

It's always terrifying to release a book into the world. You don't know whether people will love it or hate it, but either way, you at least hope they *read* it.

Thank you so much for taking a chance on this author and grabbing my new series

Accidentally Magical at Midlife?

This series is planned for 8 books, so make sure you've signed up for my newsletter to be notified of releases!

Also, I'm hard at work the next books at present. I can't wait to share them with you!

- Mel

WANT A FREE BOOK?

MELINDA CHASE

Join Melinda's Newsletter and Claim Your Freebie!
Potions and Pearls

ALSO BY MELINDA CHASE

Midlife Mayhem Series

1. *Forty, Fabulous and . . . Fae?*

2. *Divorce, Divination and . . . Destiny?*

3. *Spandex, Spells and . . . Shadows?*

4. *Paranoia, Pixies and . . . Prophecies?*

5. *Heels, Hexes and . . . Heirlooms?*

6. *Truths, Tricks and . . . Traitors?*

7. *Myths, Mysteries and . . . Monsters?*

8. *TBA*

Accidentally Magical at Midlife?

1. *Gone with The Witches*

2. *Some Like it Hexed*

3. *Gentlemen Prefer Broomsticks*

4. *TBA Coming June 2021*

5. *TBA - Coming July 2021*

6. *TBA*

I

FREE PREVIEW: FORTY, FABULOUS AND...FAE?

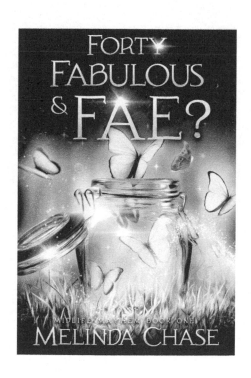

MIDLIFE MAYHEM BOOK ONE

No one expects their happily-ever-after to end at forty—but here I am one Prince Charming short of a fairytale.

Living back at Mom's place with her and Gram is not how this ex district attorney intended to start the next chapter of her life, but I shouldn't be surprised it's where I ended up.

You see, my family is cursed. *Literally.*

At least that's what both Gram and Mom claim. I've never given much thought to their ridiculous superstitions, but when three local patrons from my mom's occult shop end up dead, even I'm a bit unnerved.

So, I decide to dive right into the crazy headfirst. And what I thought would be the end of my journey…may only be the beginning.

1

"TAKE THE STUPID SHOES!" I screeched, while simultaneously launching my hardly worn pair of Louboutin's straight at my husband's head.

Ex-husband. I needed to start remembering that tiny, yet very significant detail.

To my absolute horror, Kenneth managed to duck, and narrowly avoided getting stabbed in the eye with the very sharp, stupidly irresponsible, and impossible to wear heel.

If only I had learned to throw when I was a child. Maybe that moment would have turned out differently.

But I guess I should back up a little bit.

My name is Shannon McCarthy. A boring name for a boring woman. And even more boring? Here I am, barely forty, the victim of a male midlife crisis, newly divorced, and forced to move back home to Portland, Oregon. Well, not forced. But right now, Portland seemed like a much better choice than Boston, where news of my husband's affair still littered the front pages of our local newspaper.

Who would have thought my life would turn out like this?

Not me, that's for damn sure. When I married Kenneth, with his smooth tan skin and devilish good looks, I really thought that was it for me. This was the guy I'd spend the rest of my life with. We'd have two very high profile careers, me as a D.A., and him as a judge, live in a big fancy house with a purebred Golden Retriever who listened to our every single command, and drive shiny new sports cars, like a Lamborghini, to and from our high-paying jobs every day. It was the life every single Boston girl dreams of.

And apparently, it was a life I no longer got to have. Not since Kenneth decided his pretty, young clerk was the place he should stick his junk, instead of being a respectable man and coming home to his wife.

So, here we were. I was in the middle of packing up the home we'd bought ten years ago, the one we were supposed to grow old in, while Kenneth sat on his butt and complained about every single thing I tried to box up. Anything he had bought me during the fifteen years we'd been married was apparently just a reminder of how much he had "given" me over the years.

As if I hadn't given him anything, too. I was the one who'd worked my tiny little butt off to put him through law school when I was on a public defender's salary, saving and pinching every penny I possibly could so that we didn't go hungry while he attended Northeastern.

"I should have sent you to Suffolk," I growled at him. "At least then, I wouldn't have wasted a hundred grand so you could be a corrupt judge."

"I am not a corrupt judge!" Kenneth hollered. "What part of this don't you get?"

"All of it!" I shrieked. "How could you throw away fifteen years of marriage for a fling? Fifteen years, Kenneth! We were building a life together. We were supposed to have—"

"Have what, Shannon?" he demanded, stepping up into my personal space. Those deep brown eyes of his bore into my green ones with a fury I'd only seen him use on the worst criminals, the ones he absolutely loathed and could never be impartial to.

I guessed I fell into that category now. The category of "People Kenneth Loathes."

"Have… it!" I sputtered as I attempted to articulate just what "it" was. But I couldn't find the words. "It" was huge. "It" encompassed so much that I couldn't possibly do it justice with a few shouted sentences.

"Yeah," Kenneth sneered. "'It' being the fancy house, the nice car, the dog."

Kenneth pointed an accusatory finger at Marley, our mutt. We weren't exactly able to spring for the Golden Retriever six years before.

"What's wrong with that?" I demanded. "I wanted a nice life, a comfortable one. I wanted to be happy in my marriage, unlike every other woman in my family. Is that too much to ask?"

Kenneth stopped. A brief flash of humanity leapt into his eyes, but then it was gone just as quickly. I almost wasn't sure if it had actually been there in the first place.

"Maybe it is," he finally whispered, his eyes downcast. "Because by asking for it, you tried to mold me into something I'm not… Something I could never be for you."

"All I asked was for you to love me," I murmured. Tears pricked my eyes, and I felt the brick wall I'd so carefully built in the last two weeks start to crumble and fall.

"No, you didn't." He shook his head and adjusted his navy blue tie. "You asked me to be this monument of a husband—like I was some character in a storybook. This isn't a story, Shan."

"It's our story," I insisted. I stepped up to him and cupped his soft, warm cheeks in my hands the way I always used to, begging him to look up at me.

To love me.

But he didn't. Kenneth leaned into my touch one last time before he shoved my hands off of him and stepped back, teary eyed.

"It's your story," he replied. "I have to go live my own story. And you're just not in it. I'm sorry. Really."

And I could see that he was. He thought that his apology was enough to make me forget that after fifteen years, he'd come home one night and just asked me for a divorce. Just like that. No nonsense, no lead in.

Kenneth started to walk down the giant, carpeted staircase, making a beeline for the door. I did my best to force myself to stay put. I couldn't watch him leave this time.

But my feet had other plans. Before I knew it, I was out of our enormous master bedroom and pressed up against the railing of our second floor landing.

"Ken?" I called out, right as his hand went to open our massive oak front door.

He froze, hand in the air, and didn't turn back to me.

"What?"

"Why her?" I couldn't help it. I needed to know what was so much better about this other woman. What made her worthy of breaking up a marriage?

Kenneth sucked in a huge breath, and then sighed. He didn't turn to look back at me when he spoke. I wasn't sure if it was because he couldn't bear to see the look on my face, or if he didn't want me to see the look on his.

"She and I want to live the same story, Shannon."

With that, the door slammed shut with a sound of such finality, I swear it could have happened in a Hitchcock movie.

The scream that ripped from my throat was so feral and animalistic, it almost sounded like a banshee. Not that I believed in those sorts of things.

When all of the sound had made its way out of me, and my vocal chords had been just about rubbed dry, I slowly turned back to the bedroom, where I had about fifteen boxes full of clothes to seal and pack.

Except they were all done.

Every single box that I had packed up was closed and sealed nicely with two layers of tape, as if some invisible assistant had come along and finished the task for me in mere moments.

For a second, my heart stopped, and my heavy panting caught in my throat.

"You're imagining things, Shannon," I muttered to myself. "You must have closed those boxes already."

But how could I have? The last thing I remembered doing was yanking a Louboutin out of an open box to throw at Kenneth. Even the box of shoes, though, was closed and sealed.

Freaked out, I headed down to the kitchen to finish packing. The movers would be coming in the morning, and I'd be on a flight home the next afternoon.

Home.

I hadn't been there for more than a brief, two-day visit in nearly ten years. It wasn't that I didn't love my mom and my Grams, or Grams' best friend, Dina. I loved them more than words could say.

It was their beliefs I didn't love. All three of them were impossibly superstitious, and whenever I was around, I always felt like there was some big secret I was missing out on, some sort of major thing I just didn't know.

Which was crazy. They were my family, and I knew everything there was to know about them all.

But still. My intuition always went haywire whenever I was in that house, the same one Mom had grown up in after her father had abandoned them.

The same one I'd grown up in.

Less than twenty-four hours after my final fight with Kenneth, I was in an Uber and on my way to the airport.

And stuck in traffic.

"Are you sure there are no backroads you can take to get us there faster?" I asked the driver, a stout young man with fire engine red hair, the same color as mine. He had a South Boston accent, and drove with his golfing hat on backwards.

"No, lady, sorry," the guy shrugged. "Traffic's real bad out today, huh?"

"Sure is," I sighed, and looked at my watch for the fifth time in as many minutes.

I had half an hour before the gates closed, I missed my flight, and I was stuck in Boston for... who knew how long. I just needed to get out, to go home and see my family and make some sort of attempt to reconnect with life itself. Figure out my next act.

Without Kenneth.

The traffic didn't improve, even by a smidgeon. I was late to the airport, and by the time I made it through security, I was sweaty and anxious as I sprinted through the terminal.

Just as I got up to my gate, I saw those big white doors start to close.

"No, wait!" I screamed, so loudly I turned a plethora of heads. The attendant either didn't hear me or didn't care, because those doors closed all the same.

"I... have... a ticket... for this flight," I gasped at the cranky old flight attendant manning the door. "I need to get on."

She looked up, appraised me with dark hazel eyes, and then shook her head with absolutely no remorse.

"Sorry," she shrugged. "Can't help ya. Get here earlier next time, like everyone else."

"No, look, you don't understand," I wailed. I could already feel it all coming down on top of me, revving up for a massive breakdown. The cheating, the divorce, the move, the pre-mid-life crisis I was about to have. "I'm getting a divorce, okay? Because my cheating ex-husband has some grand idea that he's going to go live a story, whatever that means. But he's not just living a story. Oh, no. He is living it with *someone else.* The man cheated on me and then had the gall to blame it on this insane need to 'live my own story.' What does that even mean? Do you know? Because I don't. I just… don't. So anyways, now I'm here, trying to get on this flight to go home and see my Mom and my Grams—who I haven't seen since Christmas, mind you. I am a terrible daughter, I know, save it. My ex used to tell me that all the time. He also said I was a terrible spouse, but he's the one who cheated, so you tell me who got the last word there, okay? All I'm really saying is that I need, and I mean *need,* to get on this flight and get the hell out of this city before the whole thing falls down and suffocates me. So is that too much to ask, for you to open those doors and let me get on my flight so I don't suffocate?"

Yeah.

It wasn't until after I'd finished, and felt that sort of out of breath panic a person feels after they've acted like a total idiot, that I realized I'd pretty much just dumped my entire life story on a total stranger.

And an entire airport terminal.

The stewardess, though, looked wholly unimpressed and unamused with my story. She just shook her head and sighed.

"Go back to customer service and they'll get you on the next flight," she informed me. "Have a good day."

She glanced back down at whatever stupid paper was on her desk, and that was when I lost it.

"Listen to me!" I hissed, crouching down so I could meet her eyes head on. "You need to let me on that flight. Now."

All of a sudden, the woman's hazel eyes went blank, kind of like a person's does in an over-acted TV scene where they're supposed to be hypnotized. She stared at me, and this scary smile twitched the corner of her lips, but didn't go all the way, and sure as hell didn't meet her eyes.

"Okay, you can get on this flight," she said

robotically, and then went to open the doors as if she was a puppet on a string.

I didn't even have time to question the strange oddity. I just nodded my thanks and rushed past her to get on that plane.

Keep Reading
Grab Your Copy Here!

ABOUT THE AUTHOR

Melinda Chase is an author of Paranormal Women's Fiction.

Over forty years young, Melinda loves writing tales that prove life—romance—and 'happily-ever-afters'—***do exist*** beyond your twenties!

Her debut Series, *Midlife Mayhem* is a snarky, hilarious, romantic adventure, sure to please fans of traditional paranormal romance and cozy paranormal mysteries!

Join Her Newsletter Here!

Made in the USA
Las Vegas, NV
28 September 2021

31281331R00152